THE MERMAID OF ELLIS PRIME

and other short stories

STEPHANNIE TALLENT

This is a work of fiction. Names, characters, places, and incidents either are the product of the author's imagination or are used fictitiously. Any resemblance to actual persons, living or dead, events, or locales is entirely coincidental.

For more information, contact: stephannie@stephannietallent.com

First e-Book edition September 2021

ebook ISBN: 978-1-942655-27-5
Print ISBN: 978-1-942655-28-2

www.stephannietallent.com

To my mother-in-law Rosemary and my father-in-law Curtis: the best in-laws a woman could want!

CONTENTS

Introduction   vii

The Medic of the Crow City Mining Co-op   1
Everything Except Humans   16
The First Day In Her New Life   22
I'm the Maintenance Man   35
The Death of Workshop Betty   48
Of Parrots and Pigeons   58
The Death of Innocents   67
The Mermaid of Ellis Prime   79

About the Author   91
Also by Stephannie Tallent   93

INTRODUCTION

Aliens. Different worlds. Earth now, and Earth in the future. These stories range from close to far.

I wrote *The Medic of the Crow City Mining Co-op* during an intense SF workshop in Las Vegas. As part of the workshop, we visited Springs Preserve to glean inspiration for our story.

From the Springs Preserve website: *Springs Preserve is a 180-acre cultural institution designed to commemorate Las Vegas' dynamic history and to provide a vision for a sustainable future.*

I'd learned, even before reading the essays and displays, of the devastating (and ongoing) impact of our use and manipulation of the Colorado River. I was really intrigued by the short film on the construction of the Hoover Dam. The scope of the project, diverting the river, the amount of materials, all completed with the technology of nearly 100 years ago, fascinated me.

I remembered the statement about losing more than a hundred good men during the construction, and decided to make my main character, Miri, a doctor working at the site in my story.

Springs Preserve also has wildlife exhibits. The little gray fox, curled up in his human-created den, directly influenced my alien Regits.

And the pink crystals? I've no idea where *that* came from. Unless Vegas, ooh, shiny. One of the check in women at Main Street had sparkly peachy pink eyeshadow, expertly applied. Maybe that stuck with me.

www.springspreserve.org

What does an alien do when they are sick? Find out in *Everything Except Humans*.

For what it's worth, I've never had a client take off their clothes in the exam room—but I *have* heard about it happening.

Sometimes our lives don't follow the path we've planned. (Certainly all of us have experienced that with the COVID-19 pandemic.) Shadi, a newly licensed telepathic Operator from a privileged background, finds her life going in a completely different direction than she expected.

I'm the Maintenance Man and *The Death of Workshop Betty* take place in a dystopian near future, where nanotechnology enables various body and skill modifications. The latter takes place first chronologically, but it's best to read them in the order presented here.

Of Parrots and Pigeons was written during a short story workshop, with the direction that your hometown was under siege or invaded from something on a set list; and your protagonist was from that same list. Trust me, the choices were both varied and strange. It, like many of the stories in this collection, has an ecological bent.

What if you had a super spy, James Bond-like character in space? *The Death of Innocents* features a talented, cold agent with a code of honor all her own.

The title story, *The Mermaid of Ellis Prime*, is a story with an undercurrent of consent. We do things to animals all the time: eat them, keep them as pets, house them in zoos, and more. We tell ourselves some of these things, at least, are in their best interest. But we don't ask them.

But it is also a story of hope, and building bridges, between species. I hope you enjoy the collection.

THE MEDIC OF THE CROW CITY MINING CO-OP

MIRI PLACED HER BATTERED ALUMINUM LUNCH TRAY ON THE EMPTY plastiform table in the far corner of the canvas-covered crew mess area.

Everywhere was loud: good-natured shouting and guffaws from the crews, the clanks and whirs of the drilling machines, the high-pitched whine of the generators.

The corner seemed quietest.

The white table was so coated with fine dust it looked pink. She ran a finger through it. Powdery. It would get everywhere. Pores, eyes, lungs. Probably cause cancer ten years down the road, but none of the miners wore masks or respirators.

Just breathed it all in.

Sure, most cancers were curable, but cancer still sucked. No sense in complacency.

Mining crews and other workers of the Crow City Mining Co-op crowded around most of the tables in the mess area. Miri identified at least five different distinct languages that she herself spoke, and a jumble that she didn't. If she sat by herself, she could focus, block out the cacophony, acclimatize.

"Good luck," her Assignments Officer had said drily before she flew out. "Last camp medic quit within two weeks, forfeiting all her regular pay on top of the hazard bennies. Try not to piss off the bosses, this time, and I'll get you somewhere nice for the next assignment."

Promises, promises. She was beholden to the Planetary Personnel Workforce, the PPW (or Pew Pew, when she was feeling particularly grumpy), for another five years, for paying for her medical degree. She'd already served ten. She knew the score.

Miri stepped over the plastiform bench and eased herself down, stretching her long, travel-sore legs out in front of her. She'd grabbed a bowl of some sort of chowder from one of the bins in the center of the mess, not even caring what it was. Protomeat, vege, native roadkill. Who cared. Planet hopping always threw off her stomach, and the change from stale recycled ship's air to a planet side atmosphere numbed her taste buds anyway.

And this atmosphere...she could feel her lips chapping. Hot and dusty and mummifyingly dry. The shade from the canvas awning did little to cool off the mess hall, just kept the crews from blistering in the mid-day sun. The camp was centered in a narrow canyon, one of many side canyons in this maze of badlands, off the main canyon, the site of the actual mining, but the three hundred meter tall, glowing red and pink cliffs couldn't block the overhead sun.

Some enterprising soul had hung some fluid-soaked cotton sheets up as an impromptu swamp cooler, but the pungent scent wafting from them with every gust of wind made her wonder what the liquid was.

Hell, she wasn't wondering.

Someone pissed on 'em. Probably thought it was funny.

Guess there was enough water to not worry about recycling urine. Of course, the river in the main canyon was the whole bugaboo in this op, from her quick reading on the transit over. Rare minerals, river in the way, move it over and dig to high holy hell, damn the consequences to any native species.

Story of every low-tech exploited world.

No wonder she was grumpy all the time.

Five years. Just five more years.

She dipped her spoon (also bent, pitted, aluminum, must be cheap, here) into the chowder. Took a taste.

Spat it out and grabbed her water canteen, knowing the water would just push the vicious heat closer to her tongue but needing to do *something*.

High holy fuck, what the hell did they put in there? Some native pepper ten times hotter than a freakin' ghost chili?

"Doc! Hey, DOC!"

Miri kept her watering eyes downcast. God, no. Just no.

"Doc! Who'd you piss off, to get posted here?" Jimmy Two Dogs plopped on the bench across from here, all two meters tall and hundred fifty kilos of him. His long red hair was pulled back in a stringy ponytail. Dirt creased the lines in his tanned face, aging him thirty years. "Long time no see!"

Not long enough. She'd met Jimmy Two Dogs four years ago. 0935-Orion, asteroid mining operation. A one year assignment that had felt like ten.

She got in trouble *there* when she joined with the striking miners. Jimmy Two Dogs had been their leader.

What else was she supposed to do? The miners were her friends, and they were dying because of fucking cheap ass faulty bichlorbutylene explosives and other piece-of-crap, lowest-bidder equipment.

Jimmy Two Dogs was a great guy.

Just really, really loud.

And who had she pissed off, this last time? Who *hadn't* she? She'd run out of fingers and toes if she tried to count them all, and space travel had gifted Miri's momma with a mutation that gave her daughter Miri six dexterous fingers on each hand.

"Hey, Jimmy. Keeping out of trouble?"

"What do you think, Doc? I'm here, ain't I?" He laughed loudly, then started hacking, pulling up big globs of rosy dust-streaked phlegm. "Lots of work for ya here, Doc. Lots of work. The mother fucking dust on top a the routine crap dealin' with this much blasting and pouring."

His dark eyes grew serious. "And the Yappers. Some accidents...they just ain't normal. The Yappers have something to do with the problems here. The guys know it, the bosses won't admit it. You watch out, Doc."

"The Yappers?"

"Little foxy natives. Regits, they call themselves. Cute as fuck, but nasty tempers. Poisonous fangs like a viper. Yap like the coyotes back home. Yappers." He leaned back, eyed her bowl. "You ain't gonna eat that stew, are ya? Let me take it off your hands. Go get some of the yellow stuff. Better for prissy white gals like you. Won't set your gut on fire."

"Yeah, yeah," Miri muttered. Who the fuck was he calling prissy? Jimmy Two Dogs had more curves than she did, with her nearly two meter tall, leanly muscled body. And yeah, she kept her curly, gray-streaked brown hair long, but that was just because it was easier to pin it up in a messy bun than get it trimmed all the time.

She passed him her stew. She wasn't hungry anyway.

What the fuck had she gotten herself into this time?

———

THE CLINIC WAS MORE POORLY STOCKED than she'd anticipated. And it wasn't like she was an optimistic, glass half full kind of gal.

Two modified shipping containers, insulated and air conditioned, thank the gods, formed the clinic. It had running water and electricity. She shouldn't have to note that, but she'd actually reported once to a unit that lacked those amenities.

The irregular hum and creaks of the air conditioner suggested it needed a tune up. Add that to the list.

One container included a small sterile surgery suite in the center. A stasis storage room was adjacent to the surgery suite, with five coffin-like padded support boxes for patients who needed shipment off-world to a full medical facility. All were currently empty. On the opposite end of the container was a non-sterile treatment room, with two patient treatment stations.

The other container had an examination room, two storage rooms with chipped plastiwood cabinetry lining the walls, and a small room at the end far end she could use as living quarters. It contained a stripped twin mattress on a simple aluminum bed frame and the plastiform desk and chair. An ancient comms terminal took up most of the desk, with a dusty monitor and a small detached keyboard.

A small ultrasonic shower and a narrow closet with a few bent hangers hanging off an aluminum clothes bar filled the back wall. A small plastiwood cabinet, storage for personal items, sat under the aluminum clothes bar. Neatly folded, but dusty, sheets and a lumpy pillow sat on top of the cabinet.

She'd eat in the mess. Take a water-based shower once a week, rely on the ultrasonic for day to day.

That made the set up better than some of the posts she'd drawn.

But beyond the physical layout...when she started opening storage cabinets, all she found was dust. Pink dust, despite the negative air flow integrated into the air system, that should have kept the dust out. The whole clinic smelled of the faint sulfur, like the cliffs.

Like this whole damn planet, far as she could tell.

Well, at least she didn't have a lot of crap she couldn't use taking up space.

She finally found one cabinet that had some supplies. A couple bottles of antibiotics, some pain control patches, a couple bottles of anesthetics for the inhalant anesthetic machine, a couple boxes of sterile bandaging material.

She made a mental list of everything she'd need to order. She expected the site had a lot of physical trauma injuries. More antibiotics, pain management, anesthetics. Wound care materials, bandaging supplies, casting supplies. She doubted the Co-op would spring for an on-site regenerator, or a quick healing unit, or a full body scanner, but she could ask. It was probably cheaper to hire new workers and ship off the old broken ones than maintain high tech medical equipment.

This felt more like a forward triage set up than a permanent clinic.

That meant people would die, had been dying, even with the stasis units, if it was as bad as Jimmy Two Dogs said.

She'd do her best. That's all she could do.

All she ever did.

———

SHE HEADED towards the Co-op on-site headquarters, slogging through the pink sand, keeping to the shade of the sheer canyon walls. First thing: discuss (yeah, that was the term she wanted, not *order*, not *demand*) what she needed for the clinic. Second, find out how many nurses and assistants she had floating around (she suspected the number was zero). Oh, and to introduce herself like a proper professional to the camp commander, Brugart. Can't forget that.

The concussive force of an explosion punched her in the gut.

Then screams, echoing, bouncing, off the maze of canyon walls. Human screams.

And a shrill yipping, barking. Yapping.

She could also hear, or sense, a low thrumming shriek, that made her ears ache, so much she clapped her hands over her ears and pressed just to make it stop.

The cliff sides were vibrating.

Fist-sized jagged red and peach rocks, studded with pink crystals, broke free from the cliffs and tumbled down, the crystals ringing as they impacted the cliff side, shaking more dust into the air. Miri slogged through the sand to the center of the canyon, heedless of the blistering sunlight, heedless of the crowd of workers spilling like ants out of the mess tent, HQ, and the nearby recreation and living tents.

Last thing she needed was to get killed by a rock on her first day. "What the *fuck*," she said, coughing. The pink dust filled her mouth, burning with sharp stabs of sulfur.

Which way? She couldn't tell, with everyone shoving and running and yelling.

A plume of pink dust mushroomed overhead in the seconds it took it to clear the canyon walls.

Someone grabbed her arm, began dragging her down canyon. Towards the main operation. Towards the site of the explosion.

Handed her a water-soaked kerchief that she tied over her mouth. Her coughing eased.

Jimmy Two Dogs, his dark eyes anxious.

"Come on, Doc!" he urged. "Those guys are gonna need you!"

They ran.

———

TRIAGE MODE.

Broken arms, broken legs, broken ribs. They could wait. Don't listen to the screams. Skull crushed. Three of those. Sorry, guys. Torn off limbs, ripped open guts. Ignore the reek of leaking feces, the acrid stench of burning chlorine, rubber and plastic from the explosives.

Too late for him, him, and that one—but her, she might make it.

Jimmy tied a tourniquet, using his size triple X overshirt, at Miri's direction, high up on the stump of the woman's leg. The arterial spurting slowed, stopped.

Gods above, what Miri wouldn't do for a regenerator. Or a couple dozen more stasis units.

As Miri walked amongst the body parts and blood and jagged rocks and the mist of blowing dust, an Angel of Death in a lightweight rip stop camo jumpsuit passing judgment, Jimmy yelled and hustled and organized a crew to follow her orders.

Turn him over—aw, shit, never mind. Back of the head gone.

And that was that. At least thirty dead, and a few more she knew wouldn't even make it to the stasis boxes. No regenerator and dozens who needed one ASAP.

And there, at the edge of the debris, a small furry form, maybe a meter long, a meter and a half if you included the bushy tail. Pricked ears, a black button nose at the end of a delicate pointed snout, sharp pointed teeth that she bet were the venomous fangs, and plush dusty gray fur, like a little fox. Its eyes, either side of that little snout, were tightly shut.

It curled in on itself, dark blue blood leaking from somewhere under its body, pooling under it and staining the loose linen tunic it wore purple.

Its blood smelled like sugary copper, even in the sulfur and rubber explosive haze.

A Regit. Native sentient species. What Jimmy and everyone else called a Yapper.

There was something else to that smell...not the Regit, who

smelled better than most dogs she'd met, but the explosives...that chlorine, rubbery smell....

The Regit opened its eyes, huge indigo eyes with a star-shaped pupil. Stared at her fearlessly.

Reached out one delicate, clawed hand.

Miri bent down and reached back, grasped the little hand gently. The Regit's hand was so small it only took four of her six fingers, to hold it.

She had no freaking idea how to treat a Yapper. Regit. A *Regit*.

Call it by its chosen species name, not some derogatory term.

And treatment? *Common sense, girl. Use your head.*

"Are you alright—" she started, even as she visually assessed the Yap—*Regit*. Steady breathing, the pool of blood was—*was it actually receding? was the Regit actually resorbing it? —wow, that was so freaking cool*!

The indigo eyes grew brighter and the grip on her fingers stronger.

"Aid, help, assist," the Regit said, its voice high pitched and breathy.

"I will," Miri promised. She didn't know if it was in pain or if always squeaked. No wonder the Co-op dismissed the Regits. Tiny, cute, fluffy creature, it looked more like a stuffed toy than a sentient being.

All she knew, she had to help it.

"Take that creature into custody."

Miri stood and turned. Her eyes flicked to the nametag on the man's camo jumpsuit. M.A. Brugart. Lovely. The camp commander. What a way to meet him.

Brugart was a beefy man, with bulging biceps and thighs stretching out the fabric of his uniform. Narrow pale brown eyes over chiseled cheekbones. A raised, jagged scar bisected his left eyebrow and trailed around his left eye, pulling the outer corner of his lids down, skewing his regular features. The scar dribbled out on his cheek. His salt and pepper hair was buzzed in a high and tight cut, so short that she bet his head was perpetually sunburnt.

Someone was living out their military fantasies.

"Nope, sorry, it's my patient," Miri said. "Article 15b, paragraph 66a.

Anyone under the care of official medical staff remains there until released by the doctor in charge.

"Me."

Fuck you, you jumped up 'roided out autocrat.

"Shouldn't you be doing something to figure out what happened here?" Miri added.

He purpled. Miri marveled. She'd never seen anyone ever do that before. 'Least not someone not strangled.

"Should I add blood pressure meds to my list of requested supplies?" She bent down and scooped up the Regit. It weighed less than twenty kilos. Its tunic made a soft clacking noise; she hadn't noticed earlier, but the tunic primarily consisted of pockets, stuffed with all sorts of things. Rocks, chunks of wood, who knew what else. Made sense. A furred being wouldn't need clothing in this sort of climate, but everyone used pockets.

Up close, the Regit's sugar sweet smell was even stronger, with an underscent of vanilla musk.

"Get out of my sight," Brugart said, his voice low. "I know what happened here. Those animals blew up my mining operation. Just get the fuck out of my site. And if that creature escapes, it's on you."

———

MIRI CARRIED the Regit back to her clinic, cradled against her chest. Jimmy Two Dogs, bless him, had organized a small crew of workers to clean off the mess tables and lay out the less injured victims.

They'd laid out dead behind the mess tent, away from her clinic.

Someone had yanked down the urine soaked sheets cooling the mess tent and covered the rows of bodies. Miri knew no disrespect was intended. The sheets were handy, and the survivors didn't need to see their mangled dead friends. And anyone who had thought it was funny to piss on the sheets, instead of taking the sheets to the water buffalo, a truck with a water tank, and soaking them there with actual *water* out of the *water* storage truck, was either sorry or dead themselves.

"Hey, Doc," Jimmy Two Dogs said, as she quickly surveyed the victims. He'd done a good job.

"Hey, Jimmy. Worst cases off in the clinic?" she asked.

"Yeah. I rounded up some guys who'd done field medicine before. They got some IV lines going, some morphine, in the worst of 'em. Doc, we don't got enough supplies."

"I know, Jimmy. I'll figure out something."

"Doc, watch yourself," he said, nodding at the Regit in her arms. "That little guy isn't going to be very popular around here."

"The Regits didn't set off the explosion, Jimmy. Did you smell the bichlorbutylene?" That chlorinated rubber smell. Last time she smelled it was on 0935-Orion.

When *that* mining company bought cheap ass explosives and killed two hundred miners.

Things never changed.

Jimmy Two Dog's eyes widened.

"Holy shit, Doc. Fuck. You're right. Something always, uh, stank about this op." He winced. "Sorry."

"I got work to do, Jimmy. But tonight, let's you and I meet up. I need to see the plans for this operation. I'm hoping you can help me retrieve them."

———

SHE JURY-RIGGED the stasis boxes to hold two people each. Jimmy Two Dogs kept referring to the guys, but in reality, half the miners and workers were female.

If she stacked a smaller person, male or female, with a larger (usually) male, she got twice the use out of each box.

And potentially saved five lives.

She lost half a dozen regardless. And a couple more might not make it.

Jimmy had found some good help for her, but she was short ten operating rooms, twenty surgeons, and twice that many nurses and techs, and who knew how much in supplies, meds and materials.

She did the best she could.

She'd let the little Yapper—the *Regit*—curl up on her bunk. It—he —seemed like he just needed rest and time to heal. Remarkable being.

By the time she'd finished in the clinic, it was nearly dawn. She wouldn't have much time to break into HQ, look for the reports she needed to find.

She met Jimmy Two Dogs just outside the clinic. The camp was quiet. The winds that had blown dust everywhere early had stopped, and the air was clear, free of dust. And it was freaking cold. Goosebumps pimpled her arms.

The cliffs glittered in the glow of moonlight. Three moons, she remembered, but only one was up the sky, a sharp crescent against the velvet dark sky straight overhead. This deep in the canyon, she couldn't see any hint of dawn.

Sugar spun vanilla tickled her nose. The Regit stood beside her. His star-shaped pupils had dilated in the darkness, making his eyes look like black sapphire crystalline canyons.

A second person waited with Jimmy, dwarfed by his bulk.

"Hey, Doc," Jimmy said. "This is J.B. They hack for fun. Figured we needed to get in and out pretty damn quick, so we could use a bit of help."

Miri looked at J.B., who stared at the ground and kicked at a red rock. Average body, straight shoulder length dark hair, a symmetrical but otherwise forgettable face. They'd be ignored wherever they went. Useful, that.

"Okay, thanks," Miri said.

The four of them walked to headquarters, Miri warming up with the exertion of slogging through the soft sand. The Regit, graceful and light, walked upright, silent except for the soft clonk of items in his pockets.

"What do you carry?" Miri asked.

The Regit glanced at her, then reached into one pocket, stopped, then another. He withdraw a small flat chunk of pale wood, only a couple centimeters across, and handed it to her. It was carved with deep spirals on both sides. She rubbed her fingers over it. Otherwise smooth, sanded, no splinters. Pretty, but....

She handed it back. "It's lovely."

He refused it. "Smell," he said, his voice fluting.

She raised it to her nose. Cinnamon? The Regit motioned for her to move the chunk. She did, sniffing along it. Cinnamon segued to something deeper, richer, maybe bittersweet chocolate but she couldn't quite tell. And then, the scent changed once more, as she turned it over and smelled the other side, to a brown sugary sweetness, brown sugar and something nutty.

Art. It was a piece of art. The scent was imbued into the spiral carvings.

"I want dessert," she said, and the Regit smiled, pink tongue lolling.

"Keep it," he said in his breathy voice. She wondered how much she was missing, with her human nose, how many layers she just couldn't sense.

"Thank you," she said.

They reached HQ. It was the most permanent-appearing building in the camp, a simple pre-fab structure of insulated plastiwood and dust-etched plexi windows. It was big enough for half a dozen small offices, nothing more.

J.B. did something to the scanner and the door slid open. Quieter and more efficient than Miri's first thought, which was to bash in one of the windows, if it had just been her and Jimmy Two Dogs.

They entered the building into a center hallway that stretched the length of the building. Closed doors lined either side of the hallway. It was dark and quiet, except for their boots scuffing on the dusty gray plastitile floor.

Empty.

"Engineers are working out of that room," Jimmy said, gesturing to the second door on the right. J.B. did their magic again, and they entered.

The room was windowless, the air inside still. Miri flicked the light switch, turning on overhead lights that lit the room with a pale buttery glow. Dessert on the brain.

Two plastiform desks with high tech terminals sat in the center of the room. One entire wall was an interactive glass screen, displaying a map of the canyonlands, the course of the river....and what was marked as a Regit settlement, downriver, near where the river spread into an estuary by an ocean.

"Work's going slow," J.B. said, speaking for the first time, her voice raspy. "Regs. Have to measure impact on natives, on the Regits, before doing anything major."

"Article 45b." *Any exploitation of natural resources must be thoroughly evaluated for impact on the environment and any native species, and reassessed after each adjustment.* Miri tapped the screen. The view shifted, highlighting the mineral deposits deep under the canyons. Deep under the river.

"If the Regits weren't there, it would be easier to mine all that. And cheaper." J.B. said. "Move the river, blast everything, instead of the targeted excavations we've been doing."

"You've thought about this," Miri said.

J.B. shrugged. "Same thing happened on my home world. Happens all the time."

Miri couldn't argue with that.

"And if the Yap—the Regit were shown to be dangerous, the Co-op could fight back," Jimmy said. "Like if they were setting off bombs, to get us to leave."

The Regit yipped. "Tried to stop it," he said. "Tried."

Miri heard a soft swoosh. The front door. "Guys—"

The hall lights flickered on. Heavy steps, boots on the plastitile floor, not trying to be quiet.

Brugart.

"Well," he said, filling the doorway. "Well. I'm not surprised to see you all here."

"Brugart, your operation is in direct contradiction to Article 45b. And I'm sure we'll find actual evidence that you caused today's incident, resulting in the deaths of thirty employees, and you will be charged with—"

"Doc, shut the fuck up," Brugart said.

The Regit apparently decided enough was enough.

He ran to, and *up*, Brugart, using his fine claws to climb up Brugart like a kitten climbing curtains.

And he bit Brugart on the nose.

Brugart fell like a rock, foam dribbling between his lips, the Regit leaping clear.

"Not dead," the Regit said, with a bit of regret in his voice. "But will stay unconscious, for as long as needed. Collect your evidence, please."

———

IT WASN'T QUITE that easy. J.B. had to hack into the systems, and pull together a coherent report from all the hidden, filed away data, orders, and so on.

The Regit left, then returned with small contingency of Regits, who assisted J.B., using the maps to communicate their knowledge of their world, the destruction the operation would cause.

J.B. hacked into the comms and got that report distributed. Not just to the higher ups at Crow City Mining Co-op, but to the Interplanetary Law and Justice Agency, the ILJA.

And the news services.

Jimmy Two Dogs hunted down the bichlorbutylene explosives. Not faulty, this time, just not something the Regit could ever have accessed. Not something commonly used. Miri could never forget that acrid chlorine smell, after 0935-Orion.

Miri herself had the distasteful task of making sure Brugart didn't just die, on top of caring for all the injured workers. She stored Brugart's rigid body with the stasis boxes and assigned a watch on him. Check his vitals every three hours, clean him up so he wouldn't get bed sores, and so on. He wasn't worth any more of her time, than that.

The Regit's venom induced stasis. Nifty. Could be useful, if she could analyze it then synthesize it.

That afternoon, a shuttle arrived with a complete medical team.

And a team of military police and investigators.

———

TWO WEEKS LATER.

Miri lay on a blue towel, on a pink sand beach, the hot sun high overhead, just a floppy straw hat shading her face. The gentle lap of waves against the sand lulled her, as did the fluting voices of the juvenile Regit splashing in the bay.

Jimmy Two Dogs plopped down next to her, kicking up a dusting of sand.

"Dude, put some sunscreen on," she said, shading her eyes and looking at the sunburn reddening Jimmy's pale brown belly.

"Enjoying your day of R&R?" Jimmy said. "Isn't this great? The sun, the beach."

"It is," she agreed.

"The mining op is closing for good," he said. "Just heard from J.B."

"For the best," Miri said.

"The ILJA is working with the local Regit. They may set up some sort of cultural exchange. The Regit seem open to it. Crow City had everyone at ILJA convinced the Regit were just animals."

"They're sure cute," Miri said. "Easy to assume, when you don't want to look any deeper." She was learning the Regit had an incredible culture, filled with art. Stories. Scent-based sciences.

"You gonna stay?"

"I'd like to," Miri said. "For a bit of time, at least. My AO said my tour was for a year. So I'll be staying that long. Even if there's no mining, there will be a settlement, for the delegation to the Regit."

Sure, the Regit buildings and infrastructure didn't look like much.

But they smelled incredible.

EVERYTHING EXCEPT HUMANS

A WARM, PEANUT BUTTER-Y TRAIL DRIPPED DOWN THE CHEST OF Emily's tropical ocean and orange clown fish patterned cotton scrubs top. She swiped it up, licked her finger, then continued to chow down on her peanut butter toast as she navigated the stop and go traffic on the northbound 405, Los Angeles' busiest freeway.

Emily rolled down her window, sucking in exhaust fumes, and craned her neck out to see around the Ford Extinction SUV in front of her. Nothing but bumper to bumper cars with red brake lights cutting through the cool summer morning June Gloom fog.

She turned on the news, hoping for a traffic update.

"A flying saucer! Buzzed right over us! It hit the truck then flew off!" a guy screamed to the KCAL-9 reporter on the scene.

Typical LA craziness.

THIRTY-FIVE MINUTES LATER, Emily zipped into her parking spot at the far end of the lot. The clinic, tucked into the far corner of an aging strip mall between a Korean nail salon and an old-school greasy spoon, didn't look like much, but it was *hers*.

The glass front of the clinic sported the cheery message **We Treat Everything Except Humans!** emblazoned in peeling gold-toned letters.

Emily kept her head down, not wanting to make eye contact with any of the clients jammed into the waiting room, muttering "Sorry, sorry, traffic," as she raced past the receptionist counter; through the treatment area with its two wet tables with wire grates as the table tops and tubs underneath, shelves full of drugs and supplies, and kennels and cages lining the walls; and into her small, windowless office.

Reference and textbooks lined the shelves. Her lab coats, freshly cleaned and starched, hung on their hangers on a hook screwed into the wall. The screens of the security system, with camera shots of each exam room, the waiting room, and the back areas, were arrayed above the desk.

Someone, bless their heart, had left a full travel mug of steaming fragrant coffee next to her laptop. The computer was already on and logged in to the veterinary management system, with the schedule tab open.

All the appointment slots were full.

Emily collapsed in her office chair, her one personal indulgence at the clinic: ergonomic, adjustable ten different ways, with stain-resistant smooth leather upholstery.

She'd have to get up in ten seconds, but darn it, those ten seconds would be comfortable. She chugged some coffee. Nectar of the gods.

Geogia, her licensed tech with twenty plus years of experience and a body-building hobby, poked her head through the doorway. "Jamie has loaded Rooms 1 and 2 for you. Histories and vitals already taken, so they're ready for your exams," she said, her throaty voice calm. Georgia had three grown children, and five grandchildren, two of which she was raising. Nothing ruffled her. "We do have a new client walk-in who says it's urgent. Want him in Room 3?"

"Sure," Emily said, resigned. *Busy was good.* She stood up, stretched, then went to Room 1.

Richie Costa, a chubby twenty something who smelled muskier than his ferret Tribble, plopped Tribble on the exam table. Emily squirted a dab of a sugary vitamin paste, like crack for ferrets, on the edge of the table. Tribble immediately lapped it up with his tiny pink tongue.

"Doctor, I think he has ringworm," Richie said. "He's lost some fur, and I Googled it, and he has a weird scab, and I have an itchy area right here myself." Richie turned away, yanked down his stained sweatpants, and exposed a pimply hairy ass cheek with, yes, a large crusty ring-shaped lesion right smack in the center.

"Um, yes, you really need to go see a dermatologist," Emily stammered. "A people one. For you. I can take care of Tribble. Jamie will get you a handout for disinfecting your house, and I'll collect samples for a fungal culture. In the meantime, you can start on some topical treatment and shampoos. For Tribble. You go see your own doctor for you."

And for all that's holy, pull up your pants, she thought as she grabbed Tribble and ran out of the room.

She handed the ferret to Jamie. "I heard," Jamie said, her soft brown eyes wide. "He didn't really—"

"Oh, yes, he did," Emily said, scribbling notes rapidly in Tribble's chart. "There are things I can never, ever, un-see." She shuddered. "Treatment plan and prescriptions in the chart, thanks! Bleach Room 1."

She headed to Room 2.

Georgia grabbed her arm right before she went in and pulled her back towards the office. "There's something odd about the gentleman in 3," Georgia said. "I was watching the cameras and he hasn't moved. Seriously, he's just been standing there. Look."

Emily gazed at the screen. The emaciated man wore a tan overcoat that covered him to his glossy black shoes. A black fedora was pulled down tightly over his forehead, shielding his sunglass-covered eyes. Black leather gloves encased his hands, one held over the other in front of him.

Georgia was right. He wasn't moving. Still as a statue.

Then he cocked his head and looked straight at the camera.

Emily shrieked. She couldn't help it.

But...."I gotta do it," she said to Georgia. "Sooner I go in, sooner I take care of the problem, sooner Mr Creepy is out of here. Let Room 2 know I'll be in as soon as possible."

Georgia nodded. "I'll watch from the office."

Emily grabbed a lab coat and shrugged into it. She'd skipped a coat for the first appointment, but for this one, she wanted the armor of respectability that came with the coat.

She went into the room. The man's face, turned up towards the camera, snapped down to hers as she shut the door behind her. What skin she could see, not shielded by the glasses and hat, was smooth and tan and plastic-y, like a cheap mannequin. His lips were thin and the same color as his skin.

"I'm Dr Garcia," she said, holding out her hand. "How can I help you today?"

The man cocked his head again. "Dr Garcia?" he repeated, voice metallic and harsh and deliberate. "You give medical aid to everything except *Homo sapiens*?"

"I guess you could put it that way," Emily said, puzzled, hand still stretched out to him.

"You will come with me," he stated, grasping her hand.

And *swooshed* her away.

————

NAME A KITTEN LOKI, and he'll terrorize your household. Name a puppy Lucky, and he'll get hit by a car, eat a corn cob that gets stuck in his gut, and catch every weird disease out there.

Even *think* you're having a bad day ... and things always can get worse.

Emily, disoriented, leaned over and retched, bringing up bits of peanut butter toast, before she could even think of looking up and around.

Then she was too freaked out to retch again.

The man holding her hand? Wasn't a man. And he wasn't holding her hand with his hand, he was holding her hand with an olive green and turquoise-spotted, sticky, thick tentacle that oozed mucus over her wrist.

He wasn't wearing a tan trench coat, or black glossy shoes. Those articles of clothing apparently disappeared when he transported her. (*She*, thankfully, was still fully clothed.)

He was a lumpy, tentacle-y, green, slimy alien, about five feet tall and three feet across, softly shining in the dim interior lights of his...spaceship? She was in a small area, not much bigger than her treatment room at the clinic. Hammock-like seats hung from the ceiling, and what seemed to be a control center filled one wall.

The alien looked like a mad scientist crossed a frog and an octopus together, with a tiny beak-like mouth, sturdy muscular hind limbs, and too many to count tentacles of varying thickness in place of front limbs. Except he had way too many red and white, multi-pupiled eyes, some on stalks, all of which were swiveled towards her.

And he smelled like ... plumeria? He smelled like her beach bungalow on that heavenly trip to Costa Rica she treated herself to, three years ago, her last vacation before buying the clinic. She'd marveled at the jewel-like gleams of the poison dart frogs on twilight jungle hikes, and at the friendly octopus the dive instructor introduced her to at 130 feet deep, who came out to twine a slender orange arm around her finger. The smell, exotic and thick and sweet, relaxed and anchored her.

"You must help us," he said, voice still harshly metallic. She noted a thin metal placard held in one tentacle. The voice emanated from it.

He stepped to the side, pointing to a recumbent alien she hadn't noticed. His skin seemed dry and dull compared to that of the first alien, and his tentacles were limp.

"I have no clue what to do," Emily said.

"You must help him," insisted the first.

Frog. He seemed most like a frog. Emily didn't treat many amphibians, but she had to start somewhere.

"Do you have a tub or something we can put him in? I want to try to rehydrate him." The alien grabbed her hand and one of the tentacles of the other and *swooshed*.

Emily gagged. Nothing left to come up. Apparently being transported was not good for her vestibular system. Regardless, the three of them were in a dimly lit room with a white ceramic tub, about four feet across, in the center. "Place him in there," Emily said. "Do you have any medical fluids? Anything we can bathe him with?"

"No," the alien said. "We're scouts."

Okay, so that wasn't very comforting. Scouts ahead of an invasion? a scientific expedition? what? She couldn't dwell on that.

"I need fluids, enough to cover him. Even just saline with some sugar, some dextrose. I have some at the clinic —"

Swoosh. But this time, not of her; four cases of fluids, previously stored in treatment at the clinic, were now cluttering the floor of the spaceship. "Pour them all in with him," she directed. "And if you can multitask, get bottles of enrofloxacin and B and C vitamins. Dump them in too."

She fervently hoped, as the first alien mixed in the antibiotics and vitamins, tinting the fluids orange, that they wouldn't kill the creature.

They didn't. By the time the second alien had finished absorbing the fluids, an anxious hour or so later, his skin had brightened and his tentacles firmed.

He smelled like flowers, too, like the honeysuckle that lined the backyard fence of her tiny Long Beach rental.

"We thank you," the first said, holding out a tentacle. She grasped it, anticipating the disorientation of the *swoosh* back to the clinic.

———

SHE WAS ALONE, in Room 3. Georgia barged in. "You disappeared!" she cried, her throaty voice shrill, hugging Emily to her tightly. "I rescheduled all the other clients, but I didn't know what to do otherwise. There was a shimmer, and then you were gone."

"I think," Emily said, "we all can take the rest of the day off. But before we do, let's change that sign on the front door."

We Treat Everything *from this Earth* except Humans!

THE FIRST DAY IN HER NEW LIFE

*An Operator will only employ their power at the order of the Court to
determine the truth, not to punish.
An Operator will only employ their power under the guidance of their Factor.
An Operator will never exercise their power unmasked.*

SHADI'S FIRST DAY AS A LICENSED TELEPATHIC OPERATOR FOR THE
Helian Courts started exactly like she pictured it would.

She woke up thirty minutes early, her stomach tight with excite-
ment. As of today, she was a licensed Operator. Five years of hard
training and coursework.

The light from the twin moons of Helios still dappled her linen
coverlet, the only hint of dawn a tinge of rosy gray on the tops of the
mountains to the south. The cool breeze, redolent with the thick
heady scent of engineered tiare flowers, fluttered the sheer curtains of
her open bedroom window, and kissed her cheeks with microscopic
droplets of sweet dew. An owl-like native Tursa cooed outside her
window as it zeroed back to its nest, its night's hunting finished.

Her suite filled a quarter of the top floor of her family's home, with
views towards the snow-capped peaks through one set of windows, and
the curve of the coastline, with its broad beaches of crystalline canary

yellow sand, out the westward windows. Her parents' suite occupied half the floor, and her baby sister Krissa, an Empath in training on break from school, the other quarter. It was a large house, but intimate and comfortable.

Home.

Her mother, a retired Operator, was downstairs in the kitchen, brewing coffee so rich Shadi could taste it upstairs. Her mother's voice was a soft murmur over the clink of utensils and pans. Shadi smelled browning butter, nutty and sweet, and her mouth watered.

Hands down, her mother was making her an omelet, with chives and pungent creamy cheese, in celebration of Shadi's first day as an Operator.

Her brother Theo, who'd stayed in the downstairs guest suite overnight so he could fly Shadi to the Helian Courthouse this morning, was likely assisting. An amateur chef as well as a seasoned Factor, trained to assist telepathic Operators—her Factor, now—he grabbed any chance to dabble in the kitchen.

Her father, already at work in his study, would join them for breakfast. You didn't head one of the planet's richest families by being lazy.

Everyone in the family contributed.

And Shadi?

Telepaths were rare. Telepaths who could successfully complete their training, rarer.

And telepaths with Shadi's raw power yet fine control?

She'd overheard her instructors at University discussing her a couple weeks before she graduated.

Not spying, no, she wasn't—it was just the door to Professor Smalldon's office was ajar, and she couldn't help but overhear.

"—too much power." Shadi had never liked Professor Cannev, who taught History of the Helian Judicial System. Sounded like the feeling was mutual. "She's a troublemaker. Doesn't want to follow the rules unless she decides they're appropriate."

"Her brother can control her." Professor Smalldon's gravelly bass voice, a sharp contrast to Cannev's tenor. "Don't worry, Cannev. Look at her family. I have faith in her training, her abilities, and her moral radar."

Damn right.

Shadi got up, stretching, and pulled on black cotton leggings, a snug black cotton tank top, and low soft black leather boots. The natural fabrics, simple but luxurious, felt good against her skin. She'd put on her heavy black wool Operator's robes at the Courthouse. Her interromask was safely packed in its small ceramic-metal travel case, nestled in soft foam to protect the custom molded syn-flesh and thin tiny needles. The cermet case was enameled with a bright red compound, a universal warning on any world. No one would touch her case except for her.

She reached up to pull her hair back and laughed as she touched her smooth skull.

Her mother had shaved Shadi's head the night before.

Shadi would never have hair on her head again, not as long as she was a working Operator. Not when she needed the syn-flesh of the interromask to snug up against her flesh, so the minute needles could pierce her skin cleanly.

An interromask focused and refined a telepathic Operator's power. Their Factor guided the Operator's exploration of the subject's mind and made sure they didn't go too deep.

Order out of potential chaos. A way to harness otherwise too powerful gifts.

The only legal way a telepath could use their power.

She wouldn't miss her hair—she'd always struggled with the mass of auburn curls, resorting to twisting it up in a messy bun.

Any sacrifice was worth becoming an Operator.

Time for coffee and her omelet.

The noises from downstairs ceased.

The house shuddered. A crash like her world was falling apart.

And then Theo shouted.

And *gurgled*.

Shadi was halfway down the polished wooden stairs, skipping steps with reckless abandon, before she even processed a thought, sleepy Krissa stumbling at her heels. She ranged ahead with her mind, opening herself up to any whisper of thought—then slammed herself shut. She couldn't. She'd be forsworn.

She could hurt someone, and ten more seconds and she'd be in the kitchen, Theo sipping an espresso, it was the espresso machine that made that awful noise that just wouldn't stop—

She leaped down past the last two steps, using the banister to fling herself down the short hallway to the kitchen.

Shadi's mind amplified concrete thoughts, not emotions, but the agony emanating from the kitchen blasted her in the gut. Behind her, Krissa screamed, then thudded against the cream and crystal terrazzo tiles of the ground floor.

The glass wall of the kitchen, overlooking the courtyard with the turquoise pool and herb and vegetable boxes, was shattered into scintillating shards. A hulking figure dressed in matte black cermat armor stood against the jagged spikes still in the window frame, the strap of his plasma rifle looped around one wrist. He wore a combat helmet with an activated combat data viewer visor, orange diagrams and data flashing across the clear gray screen.

Shadi's mother lay upon the floor, a pool of blood spreading from beneath her, painting the glinting crystal chips in the terrazzo floor ruby red.

Her mother was unmoving. No rise and fall of her chest. And there was nothing, nothing, from her, no thoughts, nothing.

Theo leaned against the stove, one shiny scarlet hand pressed against his neck, blood soaking his white shirt crimson. His hand dropped as she watched, exposing the cauterized edges of the ruin of his throat as he slumped to the floor.

Shadi *felt* him die.

The armored man looked at her, tapped the side of visor with his free hand, scrolled through a couple images, and then smiled.

"Found her, Deky," he said, his voice smug.

The whine of a plasma rifle from her father's office shrilled in Shadi's ears. Another hideous final thud.

Someone was keening, shriller than the rifle blast. Krissa! At least Shadi could help her baby sister—

Shadi turned back to the hallway, but Krissa sprawled against the floor, a huge lump swelling on her head. Silent.

But breathing.

Shadi snapped her mouth shut.

The keening stopped.

"Thank the gods." A smaller man, trim in contrast to the hulking soldier, wearing a dull charcoal gray cermat chest plate over a black shirt, sleeves rolled up, and black trousers tucked into shiny black boots, stepped out of her father's office. He lacked the combat visor the soldier wore, but Shadi noticed a small earpiece tucked around his left ear, the silver bright against his space-tanned skin. His cropped hair matched the shiny silver.

He pulled the door shut behind him before Shadi could see inside. "That noise was a bit excessive."

He glanced at the bodies—Mother! Theo!—on the floor. "Oktali. You were supposed to keep one of them alive."

The bigger man—Oktali?—shrugged. "Little sis is still around."

Shadi didn't look behind her into the hallway. They couldn't see Krissa, from where they stood. Krissa could get away. Get up. Get up and hide. She projected the thoughts to Krissa, daring what she hadn't earlier, using just the tiniest bit of power.

But there was no response. A telepath could reach an unconscious person, if wearing their interromask and under the guidance of a Factor.

Shadi had neither. Her mask was upstairs in its case, and....

Theo. The shriek tried to rip out of her throat, but she throttled it back. No time to grieve.

"I am Sevast Deky," the smaller man said, arching a thin brow. "You, Shadiserra, will be coming with us."

"Fuck that shit. I'm not going anywhere."

"Oktali, find the younger sister and implant the chip."

The big man nodded.

"Oh, Oktali? Let me know when you find her. I'll give you further instructions as to the location for implantation at that time. After I've spoken with rude Shadiserra."

Oktali smiled, his teeth bright. "Of course, boss."

Sevast Deky focused on Shadi.

"Oktali sets his rifle blasts at a low energy level," he said. "Higher energy, quicker kill, but Oktali likes to perpetuate suffering. Remote explosive chips can be implanted in any location. The meat of the shoulder, or thigh, for example. Or into an eye. Well, past the eye, actually, because there wouldn't be anything left of the eye afterwards. Oktali would enjoy that."

"I'll kill you for this."

"Shadiserra. If you could, if you had that killer instinct, Oktali and I would be gibbering ruins after you blasted our brains with your power. Go ahead. I'm waiting." He stared at her, pale blue eyes impassive.

She wanted to scream in fury.

She wanted to rip into him, squeeze his skull from the inside out til that serene expression melted into terror then dull lobotomized absence, she did, but she couldn't. She was sworn to use her powers to determine the truth, as ordered by the court. Not to punish. Not to kill.

If she were forsworn, no matter the justification...Operators who broke the rules never had the opportunity to do so again.

"I have a job for you, Shadiserra. If you complete it, you and your sister will go free, and I will compensate you for your loss. For this job, I will serve as your Factor. I will supply you with a military-grade interromask. One legal interrogation. That is all I require from you."

"You can't bring my family back," she said.

"Terrible things happen to people who don't deserve it all the time, Shadiserra. You and your family have been lucky enough to have been sheltered from that. Until now. At this point, you need to consider your sister's wellbeing." He tilted his head to the side, tapped his earpiece. "You have her, Oktali?"

Oktali's voice, tinny projected through the ear piece: "I do, boss. Pretty girl."

"Well, Shadiserra?" Sevast Deky asked.

Bile rose in her throat. "I'll come with you."

"Deltoid, Oktali." He tapped the earpiece. "Come along, Shadiserra. Do realize I am the only person who can disable the explosive chip. I will do so at the end of our contract."

"I won't forget," Shadi promised, teeth gritted.

No, she wouldn't forget. Not any of this.

They would pay.

———

SHADI HADN'T REALIZED Deky would take her off world until she saw his ship *The Veles*, sitting on the flight pad of the estate. She didn't know if it mattered, if she would've said no.

She couldn't say no. Not with Krissa hostage.

The ship was long and narrow, built for both space travel and planetary atmospheric maneuverability. She noted the weapons ports on the sides. Repurposed military, she guessed.

"I'm going to puke my guts out if we're jumping," she said as Oktali hustled her up the ramp and down the short narrow corridor to the crew quarters, through the medical lab and command center. "I won't be able to do anything for you for a day after at least."

"Oktali, fetch her metaclizine from the med lab. Shadiserra, will that suffice?"

She nodded as Oktali had shoved her into a tiny sleep annex, slamming and bolting the door shut from the outside.

He returned with two tablets. No water. Slammed the door shut again.

The subsonic harmonics thrum of the Witten phasefold drive of the *The Veles* thudded against her insides as the drive powered up for a jump.

Shadi popped the two tabs of metaclizine. She didn't want to sleep, didn't want to be that helpless, but if she stayed awake during the jump, she'd be puking the whole time.

For four freakin' hours.

Every distance jump took four hours. Two to prep for the phasefold, nanoseconds in it, and two to come out in one piece where you intended. And the Witten drive vibrated intense harmonics the whole time.

No thanks.

Even the low level harmonics the drive emitted to keep passengers under constant one-g thrust turned her stomach, the few times she'd travelled off world. But she could tolerate that.

Jumps were the worst.

Shadi stretched out on the thinly padded bunk that filled most of the annex, toes touching one bare aluminum wall and fingertips the other, with both her knees and elbows still bent. And she wasn't tall.

The sleep pod stank like sour gym socks. And fear. She stared up at the low aluminum ceiling, tracing her fingers across the letters someone had scratched into it, not recognizing the language. Names? Dates? Last prayers?

Her hand dropped as the metaclizine hit her.

———

SOMEONE BANGED on her sleep pod doorway, the clanging shooting stabs of pain through her skull. "Rise and shine, sweetheart!"

The drive harmonics thrummed their one-g song. Long out of the jump, then. How long?

"Where are we?" she asked, voice thick and groggy. The bare walls of her sleep annex lacked windows or even a view screen, even assuming she'd recognize anything.

"None of your business, sweetheart. Captain's retrieved the subject."

Subject. Kidnap victim, more like. She'd slept far longer than four hours, if Sevast Deky had time to kidnap someone. Her mouth was dry and gummy, and she was adding her own stink to the sleep annex. All her muscles ached from sleeping on the cramped thin bunk.

"Give me a couple minutes. Can I have some water? Clean up?" she asked.

"Check the cabinet above the bunk," Oktali said. "Five minutes."

The built-in storage cabinet nestled in the wall above her bunk didn't contain much: two bottles of water, a vacuum sealed sanisponge, and a small bottle of unidentified tablets. She chugged one bottle of water, then savored the second. Peeling off her sweat-soaked tank, she wiped her armpits with the sanisponge, then reached into her leggings and scrubbed at her crotch. The chemical cleanser tingled against her skin. She pulled the sweat-soaked tank back on, crinkling her nose.

She didn't think she'd ever be clean. Not while on *The Veles*.

———

THE MED LAB reeked of bleach. Shadi sneezed. She hadn't noticed it when she'd boarded *The Veles*, when Oktali shoved her through it to the sleep annexes.

To her prison cell.

Now she took the time to look around. Med screens flickered against the white-enameled aluminum walls. The non-slip pebbled surface of the plastitile floor was so pristine it looked smooth in the bright lights. To her left, a military grade medical sickbed stretched along the starboard wall, pushed out enough that someone could stand on the far side. Two metal stools sat on either side of the sickbed.

An occupied sickbed. Metal wrist and ankle shackles snugged the pale bruised bare extremities of a tall, thin, tanned young man. He wore a short pale blue cotton shift, nothing else, and Shadi guessed that was for her benefit, not the man's.

Sevast Deky simply didn't want her distracted. Nothing else. He had no respect for anyone.

The man opened his eyes. Bright green irises, pupils constricted in the bright med lab lights, over high sharp cheekbones. Space-tanned skin with darker freckles across the bridge of his (a pulse of sharp pain, the memory of a straight nose reflected in a mirror, as he brushed his thick brown hair back into a knot at the nape of his neck) now-askew, swollen nose.

A small dot of brown dried blood crusted his lip.

"You missed a spot," Shadi said to Oktali.

He shrugged. "There's always more blood."

Help me. A rich baritone thought intruded into her mind.

Shadi started. Shut it down, shut it down.

"Who is this?" she asked.

Please.

"None of your concern." Sevast Deky said from behind her. She turned.

He handed her a matte black cermat case. "Your mask. I will inform you of the questions I wish answered. You will seek the answers for only those questions, and relay those answers to me. Put the mask on now."

Don't do this.

"Do not forget that I control the explosive chip implanted in your sister's thigh," Deky continued. "Put the mask on."

Shadi placed the case on the nearest stool and opened it. The charcoal gray foam was stiff, supporting the dull cream syn-flesh of the military interromask. She pulled out the mask. The syn-flesh was thick and coarse, unlike her flexible custom mask. Greasy. Heavy.

She snugged it against her face before she could think about it any further.

Braced against the chill of the antibiotic gel misting her face.

Then against the tiny needles piercing her head and face.

Shadi had long ago accustomed herself to the stomach-churning shift in her vision from physical to mental, and the tug of vital energies as an interromask linked to her, even when the interromask was the one custom created for her use. Small price.

The nausea and drain was worse with the generic military grade mask. She missed her own mask, the supple syn-flesh that molded to her face, a comforting hug after the initial shock.

She missed her family. She missed her sister.

Shadi felt Sevast Deky approach. Felt him reach for the back of exposed neck with one hand, the other ready to grip her shoulder.

The classic Factor's stance.

The interromask was eyeless, but she could sense the shapes of people, the space they occupied. Their movement.

And if she stretched, she could touch them.

Sevast Deky, impassive and focused, behind her, Oktali a mass of brutal contained violence to her right.

And the man in front of her, on the sickbed. Lieutenant Mantes a' Dorian, a xenobiologist doing research for the Dorian Consortium's gene development section. A low-level telepath himself. No partners. No children. One pet, a fluffy orange striped hovercat named Pest who picked at her kibble, refusing treats, pining until her person Mantes came home, even after a half dozen research trips.

She couldn't do this. Couldn't hurt this man, who had a freakin' *hovercat* for a pet.

But Krissa.

She had to save Krissa.

Wasn't it Krissa's shoulder, for the chip? Not her thigh?

Deltoid. That's what Sevast Deky had said at the house

Shadi stretched toward Oktali.

"Deltoid, Oktali."

She tried to reach into the big man. Into his brain, tearing in with brute strength.

She couldn't. The interromask burned against her face.

"Deltoid, Oktali."

Smoke clogged her brain. Obscured her vision. She gagged.

It wasn't real. Nothing was burning. It was just controls of the interromask.

Inhibiting her. Preventing her.

"Deltoid, Oktali."

She ripped off the mask, heedless of the needles, heedless of the fine spatter of blood as she flung the mask away. She screamed as she leaped at Oktali, grabbing the front of his jumpsuit.

She didn't wait. She didn't restrain herself. Just ripped.

The little sister sprawled on the tile, sleep shirt hiked up her thighs, trying to push herself up but slipping back down. Pretty little thing. "Deltoid, Oktali." That was it. Code to kill. Too bad. He could've had fun with this one. Rifle to cut. Quick and quiet. What a shame. Too quick, too quiet, boring. But done. Mental snapshot of baby sis's blue eyes, pupils dilating in death. Pretty.

I have faith in her moral radar.

Someone said that once.

Shadi didn't care.

She blasted Oktali's brain. Turned the contents of his skull to meaty mush. It was *easy*.

He was dead before they both hit the floor. Too quick. Shadi rolled off him, stood, and pointed at Sevast Deky.

"She's dead. Krissa. You ordered her dead. Like everyone else."

Sevast Deky backed away. "Now, Shadiserra. Don't be hasty. Do you know how to pilot this ship? First thing I did when I acquired it was disable the onboard flight AI."

"I don't care." One step closer.

"Even if someone finds the ship before it runs out of supplies, you will be tried and executed as an Operator who broke her vows."

"I don't care." She paced around him. One hand on his bare nape, one on his shoulder. Theo.

"I'll make you a partner in my intel collection enterprise. We could have an ongoing relationship as equals."

"I. Don't. Care," she breathed against his neck.

And *blasted*.

———

THE MED LAB had a chute to the ship's recycler unit. Shadi dragged both Sevast Deky and Oktali to the chute. Sevast Deky slid down easily. She had to shove at Oktali to get him to fit. But he did.

She unfastened Lieutenant a' Dorian's shackles. Didn't watch as he sat up. She poked around in the med lab cabinets until she found a couple bottles of water. She handed one to a' Dorian.

"Thank you." His real voice sounded like he had in her head. Just a little raspier.

"Do you know how to fly this thing?" she asked.

"No, but if what he said about the AI is true, I can probably repair it."

"You reached to me." Reached to her. Without a mask. Without a Factor.

A' Dorian gazed at her. "Helian, right? You guys have all sorts of rules and regulations. We don't. I mean we have rules. They're not just as rigid. We rely on a telepath's own moral compass."

She nodded.

"They would've killed me. Killed you. You did nothing wrong. You just protected us." He reached for her hand. Held it. Let the warmth of his concern wash over her. Reassuring her. Without a mask. "I'm very grateful."

"Revenge. That's why I did it. I'm unfit to serve."

He shrugged. "Maybe on Helios. But not for the Consortium. I'm going to find some clothes, then work on getting the AI online. Let me know where you want to go. I can drop you off anywhere."

Shadi watched him go, his wobbling stride gaining assurance as he headed towards the command center.

She couldn't return home.

There was no one there for her. Just a vacant house, haunted by the dead bodies of her family. Surely someone had found them by now. Surely someone was wondering where Shadi was.

And when they found her...if they found her....

Shadi didn't deserve that.

She walked to the command center. Her scalp itched. She needed to grow out her hair.

"Take me to the Consortium."

I'M THE MAINTENANCE MAN

"You don't want to do this, Kate." The man, Mr John Jefferson Mayers (according to the brass nameplate on the office door) sat at his teak desk, palms flat against the dark polished wood. He was generically handsome. Mid forties. Even features, with tiny scars from nanosculpting, only apparent to someone with *her* eyes. Rich brown hair like melted chocolate that actually looked real, not color treated, with silver frosting at the temples. So distinguished! Enhanced royal blue eyes fringed with the darkest, thickest lashes she'd ever seen.

Yum! She liked those lashes. She might try them, later.

His voice matched his face: assured, not too deep, not too high. Interesting. He wasn't scared, not really. More like *resigned*.

A computer monitor, screen flickering off, canted across one corner of the desk. A sleek keyboard sat in front of him, the keys still warm (go thermal imaging!) from his fingers typing. A steaming mug of coffee, black, no sugar, no cream, no nonsense, left a heat mark on the pristine desktop.

A metal coaster, embossed with the company logo, sat next to the mug.

Resigned, and just a bit nervous. Things out of place, a man out of time.

The office was quiet except for his breathing, twenty twenty breaths per minute, perfect vision.

Not a sound from the party, one floor down. Not the band, playing vintage 1950s tunes, the stalwart company men doing the twist, the mashed potato, with their pretty boys or girls; not the staccato conversation of verbal jousting or testosterone heated arguments; not the clink of tiny silver cocktail forks against vintage porcelain or celebratory crystal champagne flutes.

She could almost, almost, hear the beat of his heart. Thu-thud, thu-thud. Was the rate increasing? Of course it was! Why wouldn't it? Pretty Boy Floyd sitting there knew what she was.

The window behind him, glass turned to nighttime work mode, reflected the room: the desk, the plush charcoal grey velvet tufted sofa, the steel and leather office chairs. The bloody orange and red abstract art on the ghost grey walls. The gleaming terrazzo floor, flecked with grey and cream and the very rare drop of scarlet. Rubies. Lab-grown rubies embedded in his office floor.

She could see, in the reflection, above the scrolling news feed running along the bottom of the window, the tiniest of bald spots back of his head.

Nothing he'd ever have to worry about. Wasn't that nice of her?

She stood in front of his desk, posture perfect, tits up, between him and the locked windowless door. She wore a sleeveless black cocktail dress with a snug velvet bodice and a full taffeta skirt and black patent high heels so far beyond fuck me pumps *she* didn't even know how she could walk in them. Pretty!

So pretty! And suited to the party she'd just left. Blending in was something she was trained to do. She was *good* at her job.

Charming, vivacious, pretty, oh so pretty. A secretary or someone's girlfriend or just a Fancy Nancy hired for the event, wowed by the swanky party, the dashing company men, the snazzy champagne. Inconsequential in a parade of equally lovely young women, and not a few men.

The company took care of its executives.

As long as they took care of the company.

Her vivid russet curls shifted and flowed down her back, restless, wafting the scent of rosemary and mint. Calming. That scent always calmed her.

One tendril crept forward, snaking around her bare wrist, the steel cores coated with a polymer mimicking smooth silky hair.

She jumped on his desk. Mary Lou and Simone stick that landing! Leaned close to him. Put her small hands, with her pretty French manicure, on her knees. Smiled. Pearly whites to welcome him to the Pearly Gates.

"Oh, Kate," he said. "Just make sure the truth gets out."

"Truth doesn't matter, sweet thing," she said, her voice Marilyn Monroe breathy. "You're *broken*, and I'm the Maintenance Man."

———

HIS CHAIR, steel and leather, had wheels. She liked wheels. She wheeled him right over to the corner, his head lolling, the slash across his throat still oozing, those pretty blue eyes dilated and blank.

She poked at an eye, stroked the eyelashes. Wow. Those lashes were natural. She hoped he'd had kids. Genes like that should be passed on. She plucked an eyelash and swallowed it.

Her internal tech could analyze the genes, figure out how to code for the lashes. She'd be so pretty with indigo eyes and pale skin and those thick, black lashes.

The tendril of her hair, so sharp blood didn't even stick to it, rested with its fellows, now tucked into a thick knot at the base of her neck. Quiescent. How's that for the word of the day?

Her hands and arms were clean, as was her dress. One drop of blood dotted the toe of her shoe. She took it off and licked it. Put it back on. Clean as a cat. Kit-Kat Katie.

She did love her job.

"I'm a Maintenance Man, and I've cleaned a lot of spots," she sang, leaning down to type on the keyboard. The monitor hummed to life. "All over the world."

The screen began flashing, then accessed the Net drive. She pushed it hard, typing five hundred words per minute, her slender fingers a blur. The thin smell of burning electronics overcame the coppery scent of John's coagulating blood.

"Tell me your secrets, you gorgeous hunk of metal and silicon." She twitched her right eye, switching from vision to collection, the absinthe green iris brightening to chartreuse, and began recording data. Columns of red numbers against a black background appeared on the actual screen. Wow, he'd color-coordinated his display with his office decor! 3-D multicolored schematics appeared in front of the screen, scrolling from design to design so fast the gleaming colors became a rainbow blur.

She didn't read it or analyze it herself. That wasn't her job. If her scanners caught something she could fix right now, she'd be alerted, and she would fix whatever it was, but otherwise, that was up to others. Analysts and collectors and strategists.

Well, sometimes, just sometimes, she would read. Just a little. Because otherwise just standing here was boring.

She hated, hated, hated being bored.

She frowned. That was odd. Her tech flagged, then crunched, a particular column of numbers, decoding them into plain English that her human brain could understand.

Data on job modifications. Soldiers and sailors and factory workers and cops and everyone, everyone!

Including data on Maintenance Men.

Data on *her*. Her mods, her augmentations, her capabilities, her weaknesses.

They thought *she* was broken? That she was *broken*?

Why, she was the best Maintenance Man they'd ever had. Hands down, rootin' tootin', and boy oh boy was she out of here lickety-split.

She could hear death coming for her on little cat feet, nearing the office door.

Pitter patter and the click of claws.

Her hair unbound itself. Two tendrils whipped out, each slicing an arc through the reflective window behind the desk, slicing right through the ever-present news feed scrolling merrily along.

The excised circle of glass fell outward, reflecting the full moon in rotating flashes. Pretty, pretty, pretty! It wheeled down to the hover rail tracks hundreds of feet below and splintered the moon into thousands of pieces.

The office door opened.

"Kit-Kat Katie, we're a-coming for you," they sang—tiger girl Jean Jeanie and SoCal Jeffrey in his ratty bathrobe, it sounded like—"so don't run away."

Kit-Kat dove out of the window after the glass.

———

BY THE TIME she'd glided to the ground, strands of hair linked and spread out like a red sail, she'd switched her mental mods.

Buh-bye Kit-Kat Katie, hello plain Kate. The original.

Saliva, flavored by burning electronics and coppery blood, welled up in her mouth. Kate spat. Now was *not* the time to worry about what Kit-Kat, that manic pixie sociopath, had done.

Definitely not the time for her to feel sick about it.

She had the memories tucked safely away, but she didn't have to look closely at them. Not yet.

She did know she had to run. She was down on the broken concrete sidewalk, even below the hover trains of the middle class, where only refugees and transients, out of the loop of regular society, out of control, hiding from The Man, lurked. No man's land, no woman's either. The stench of garbage and excrement watered her eyes.

She had to reach a safe spot to access that data she clearly wasn't meant to see. Then she had to figure out how to convince the Company she wasn't broken, no siree, don't look at me, look the other way while I run, run, run away.

Kate. She was *Kate*. Kate, lethal Kate, smart Kate, stubborn Kate. Absolutely not whimsical Katie. Kit-Kat Katie thought Kate was boring, and boring was fine. *Boring* was necessary. *Boring* would save her life.

Boring was *not* a jaunty cocktail dress and patent pumps with five inch heels. What was Kit-Kat thinking? Kate took off the pumps, holding them up at eye level, not caring about the filthy sidewalk, the soft things underfoot squishing between her well pedicured toes.

Vintage 1990s Louboutin, with a blood red sole, for a girl with a bloody soul.

Not tech.

Not something she could modify.

She ran her fingers along the back neckline of the dress, found and scanned the label with her fingertip sensors. The image of the tag popped up in front of her right eye. *Boutique Christian Dior Paris 782977.*

Crap. Crappity-crap, don't talk smack.

Kit-Kat had exquisite taste in fashion. Execrable taste for a getaway, though.

Who wore vintage to a job?

Crazy kid twenty-three-year-old Maintenance Man Kit-Kat, that's who. Not real Kate, forty-five-year-old in her original brain Kate, in her modified to prime-of-life, late twenties body, the longest serving Maintenance Man *ever*.

No time to waste, gotta make haste. Jean Jean Jeanie, that sparkly sexy half human, half tiger, was after her. SoCal Jeffrey was a 'coming too, with his mods that really tied the room together.

Get a grip, Kate.

Gods above, she was tired. Half her brain was analyzing the data snapshot, and the tidbits it fed her consciousness weren't good, not good at all. Instability in the Matrix, London Bridge was falling down, no one could put Humpty Dumpty back together again.

Louboutins clutched in her left hand, Kate started running.

————

PARANOID DIDN'T BEGIN to describe Kate. She had her penthouse apartment, suiting a well-paid, treasured Company employee, with its views of the city and ocean. She had her mid level safe house, the one that the Company expected each and every conniving Maintenance Man to possess. She made sure the Company had found it. She'd hid it, and competently, but didn't use any finesse or flare.

Then she had two *more* safe houses, each a little dirtier, grimier, lower class, at different ends of the city. Her ownership was hidden from public records and traces and the Net, buried deep, so deep, but the safe houses occupied real space, with physical addresses. Kate thought the company might know about one of those. Maybe both.

Kit-Kat knew about both.

The only place she trusted right now? Her bolt hole, her rabbit hole, that she'd dug out herself in one night when she jacked and booted the construction worker persona and mods, tightly locking even Kit-Kat out. It wasn't on any housing record, or city schematic, or anywhere on the Net. She had a hole in her brain, from when she'd wiped any trace of the construction and engineering mods.

As far as anyone but Kate knew, the bolt hole didn't exist.

Kate ran, dodging homeless people and packs of feral dogs, splashing through puddles of piss and polluted water. Kate, herself, the real her, fully reasserted herself, banishing Maintenance Man mod Kit-Kat. And as she did so, she *remembered*.

Something was broken with the whole system of personality mods. John from R&D had found the records, hidden behind walls of fake data and corporate assurances.

John, married to her best friend from college Lily. If not for Lily, they never would have spoken. Not a Company man in R&D and a Maintenance Man. Kind of like beat cops and Internal Affairs.

But then he shared the data and his concerns with her. They both dug deeper. And what they found scared the crap out of both of them.

Hate your job? Hate how it makes you feel? Hate the fear, the monotony, the niggling sense of something just isn't right with the world but hey this will help you cope, whoa, even better, it's not like you're even there!

Job mods. A quick medical procedure, quick in and outpatient surgery, and voila! All set.

So many people opted for the mods. Years of published safety data, right? And work was so boring.

Or soul crushing, more like.

But the data....

Soldiers suffering worse than PTSD, slaughtering their families, thinking they were enemy forces.

Workers repeating their tasks, not stopping to eat, sleep, or drink, til they wasted away or had heart attacks that even nano tech couldn't fix.

And Maintenance Men, Company assassins, spilling into their prime personalities, interweaving with the real person, til they had to be put down like rabid beasts.

Including *her*.

Bolt hole.

She shoved aside the manhole cover and scrambled down the damp ladder, her bare feet steady on the rungs. Once in the sewer, ten paces to the right, ignore the muck, then tappity tap on the brick and concrete wall and that section just *shimmers*, quick quick toss in the Louboutins and jump on through, quick quick.

The wall shut behind her. Cool, fresh scented air, rosemary and mint, ruffled her hair. The russet strands wriggled with pleasure, crooning *Over the Rainbow* in their theremin voice.

She wiped off her legs with a cotton towel from the stack kept right next to the entrance just for that purpose and headed straight to the shower, stripping off the Dior as she crossed the smooth porcelain tiled floor. Lights brightened as she approached, then dimmed behind her.

The bathroom, like the rest of the safe house, was spare yet luxurious. Marble mimic floor and walls, endless hot water with power stolen from the city. The water rinsed away the stench of her exertion and fear. Rosemary and mint. Calming.

With just a hint of eucalyptus and resinous pine to energize her.

She had work to do.

She got out, dried off, tossed on a pair of snug black tech leggings and a black sports bra. Sank into the wool and steel office chair in front of her computer, connected via a dozen back doors to the Net, and typed in John's screen name.

She really had to talk to John—

Golly, Kate, I'm really sorry. So sorry. But I'm the Maintenance Man, and I had a mess to clean up. A really big mess, the Company said. And if I didn't fix everything, EVERYTHING, I'd be in heaps of trouble. Heaps!

Oh, no. No.

John and Lily's twins, Francie and Rick. Bright blue eyes with thick, thick lashes. Just ten years old. Lily, her quick smiling face and wicked wit. And John, gentle John, who cared so damn much. Her conscience. Bringing her back to human.

A message flashed across her screen.

RUN.

RUN RUN RUN RUN RUN RUN

Run run run away over the rainbow and don't look back!

Did Kit-Kat find out about this place and tell the Company? Maintenance Men were programmed to be loyal. They could and did think and act for themselves, or else Kit-Kat would've just turned herself in to Jean Jeanie and SoCal Jeffrey. But Kit-Kat also didn't think things through. If she'd found out about the bolt hole months ago, she could've let the knowledge slip without a second thought.

Creatures like Kit-Kat never thought about something more than once.

Audio monitors from outside the bolt hole caught the clang of the manhole cover being shifted.

John was dead. Dead, dead, dead, his blood seeping across his ruby-dotted office floor.

Kate couldn't let his data die with him.

She yanked on socks and boots and grabbed a tech jacket from a carved wooden wardrobe. Laptop into a tech bag. And go go go, out the back entrance hidden so carefully through the back of the wardrobe and into the sewers again, just as she heard the screech of the front door alarm.

Deep into the sewers. Look out for the alligators.

———————

NO ALLIGATORS.

Just SoCal Jeffrey, slouching knee-deep in effluvia, ratty robe open to a stained t-shirt and pj shorts, lowball glass half full in one hand.

"Gutterballs," he said. "Sorry, Kit-Kat." And tossed the glass at her, liquid spraying in a graceful arc between them.

A tendril of her hair whipped forward, slicing the glass into two pieces before it could hit her. A thicker hank formed a thin shield, blocking the drops.

Both the tendril and hank sizzled, then puffed away in caustic electronic burning, eaten up by the liquid.

"Dude," said Kate. "Duderino. That was *harsh*." She touched her head, feeling the smoothness of the missing patches of hair. Her head felt funny. Her scalp was itchy.

She ran towards him, undamaged tendrils writhing, waiting to snap.

He turned to run, but he was slow, slow as molasses, drip drip dripping down the drain, just abiding there. One tendril raked across his face, slicing his right eye; another whipped across his throat, doing what she did best, making a mess but she was gonna clean up. One last tendril ripped through his robe, his t-shirt, the flesh below, guts spilling out even as he collapsed to the ground.

Ding dong, the mean old man was dead! And she was alive, so alive!

Then her hair began falling out and her skin was on fire, burning down the house! That was no White Russian he tossed at her. What was in it, what virus, what was crawling through her skin and taking her hair, her beautiful lethal hair, Rapunzel let it down!

Kate gave up and let Kit-Kat take full control.

KIT-KAT PRESSED her hands to her skull and screamed, even as she analyzed the attack. Ooh, clever boy! The virus targeted mods, looked like. Nasty. Velociraptor claws digging into her head. She could clip those claws, and did, snicker-snack with her vorpal blade. Still, her hair, her beautiful hair, fell out in clumps, til the little that remained was just enough for a scraggly mohawk, muttering to itself.

Her scalp burned. She turned her tech's attention to it. Here's looking at you, kid, don't you want to be pretty?

Her skin smoothed and blood red stubble velveted her head as her hair regenerated, as she sloshed past Jeffrey's bring out your DEAD body.

What godawful things was she wearing, anyways? Boring boots, boring leggings, boring jacket. Well, she'd fix all that. Kit-Kat

Catwoman, that's her. Thigh high boots with stiletto heels, leather catsuit, and me-*owww*, check out these gloves. Twitch her hands just so and little diamond tipped claws click out of the fingertips.

But there's a meaner cat on the prowl. Jean Jeanie with her tiger eyes and fangs and claws. Save your nine lives, Kit-Kat, to fight another day.

Kit-Kat jogged, one eye chartreuse-bright, connecting to the city public works and tracing subterranean routes, the other dark green with a midnight pupil to see where she was going. Behind her Jean Jeanie howled, a ululating roar that tumbled cockroaches off the walls and into the sewage.

What's the plan, what's the plan? There's no bulletin board to grab names off, no china markings to shanghai.

Don't let the data die. The truth needs to get out. Everything hidden will be revealed, and everything secret *will* come out into the open.

But the Company—

The TRUTH needs to GET OUT.

Parallel to the sewers ran the landline landmines (gonna fry your mods don't even think of touching!) newsfeeds, so heavily shielded than only AUTHORIZED PERSONNEL could access them except at very special junctions.

And boring Kate was whispering sweet nothings in her ear about where one such junction might be.

But the Company—

if the newsfeeds don't tell the truth, doesn't that mean they're broken?

Kit-Kat's sexy booted feet knew where to go.

———

JEAN JEANIE BEAT HER THERE, her lambent amber eyes reflecting the red safety light above the access door. She wore a cat suit to mirror Kit-Kat's, but her feet, great tiger paws with long sharp claws, were bare. Her hands, paws with handy dandy opposable thumbs, were ungloved.

Hold that tiger, hold that tiger!

Kit-Kat tried, oh she tried, to whip a strand of hair at Jean Jeanie, but slow SoCal Jeffrey had pulled a fast one and her hair just wasn't itself yet.

No one could cut Rapunzel's hair without it growing back zippity quick, but she was a fairytale girl and not Kit-Kat, more's the pity.

Kit-Kat's strip of hair lay limply down her back. The rest would grow back in a day, but she didn't have that day.

Out of time.

Jean Jeanie chuckle purred, swiveling her tufted ears to Kit-Kit.

Darn, that tiger was *hot*, even though Kit-Kit was just seconds from being slaughtered. Fearless, too.

Jeanie had to be hot and fearless. 'Cause otherwise she wasn't the brightest crayon in the box.

What do tigers dream of, when they're waiting to kill you?

Perfect posture, tits up, Kit-Kat bold in her Catwoman suit.

Kit Kat sidled up to Jean Jeanie, cool as a cucumber, sweet as sugar, yep she was in a bread and butter pickle. But not giving up yet. Never give up, never surrender.

"Hey, Jeanie," Kit-Kat said.

"Sorry, Kit-Kat," Jeanie said, claws extending. Saliva dripped from one protruding fang.

Tame the wild beast.

"So pretty, Jeanie, so pretty," Kit-Kat said, bring up one velvet gloved hand, claws just poking out at her fingertips. "Can I touch before I die? I've always loved you."

Tigers were *vain*.

"Sure thing, Kit-Kat," she said, tilting her cheek at Kit-Kat. "Doesn't change anything."

Jeanie's paw clamped against the Kit-Kat's neck. Her paw pads were warm, warm as her rumbly purr. "Take your last touch, Kit-Kat. I'll make it quick."

Kit-Kat trailed her claws along Jeanie's velvety furred cheek.

Claws extruding Jeffrey's virus.

Tiger, tiger, burning oh so very bright.

"Sorry, Jeanie," Kit-Kat said, ducking away from Jeanie's paralyzed paw and stepping back.

She couldn't just stand over Jeanie, not as the woman howled and screamed and gurgled.

Jeanie was more tiger than human. So many many mods, for that virus to meet.

Kit-Kat, let the truth out. Fix the feeds.

She stepped over Jean Jeanie's quivering body. Jeanie's feet and hands and face were bare bone, with glistening red chunks drip drip dripping. Not so pretty anymore. Kate peeled off her gloves, dropped them onto Jeanie's torso.

The door had an access pad. *Bypass it*, Kate said

So Kit-Kat did. And then she fixed the broken feed.

'Cause she's the Maintenance Man.

———

KATE SLUMPED next to the data entry portal. John's truth was out, for millions and millions to see, scrolling across screens everywhere. Windows, billboards, vids, immersions. No one connected would miss it.

Kit-Kat was clever when it came to her job.

Nobody does it better than you, Kit-Kat, Kate murmured.

The Company would try to shut it down. They'd try, and they'd succeed, eventually, but Kate thought they wouldn't be quite fast enough. And there were other Companies, companies that would jump in like hyenas to the aftermath of the slaughter. Companies who would swear *their* mods were safe.

And she and Kit-Kat would be around, to make sure they stayed honest.

Kitten, you're the best.

THE DEATH OF WORKSHOP BETTY

HANDS REACHING UP THE COBWEB FESTOONED BARE-TIMBERED ROOF, like she could just flick off the buzzing bright fluorescent lights with one little twitch of a cuticle-torn fingertip, Betty arched her back.

Stretching. Posing.

Smirking as she saw Crip's rheumy gray eyes popping, hoping one of her shirt buttons would zing straight off from the sheer force of her magnificent bosom stretching the dull gray knit fabric.

That big sweet snaggle-toothed smile, one brown tooth askew, on his wrinkled face.

She didn't think of the sweat stains at her armholes or her blood-shot, watering eyes, stinging in the stink of rare metals and bacto-solvents.

At least ol' Crip thought she was still smoking hot.

And that made him happy.

You take what you can get, these days.

"I'mma gonna get widgetized," Crip said. "Next paycheck, I got me enough for that tear down mod. My hands'll be here, but my mind will be off on some South Seas beach banging a gal like you."

A gal like her. Fifty if she were a day, and an old fifty at that. Blond hair streaked gray, crow's feet accenting her baby blues. But Betty worked hard to keep her figure. That's all she had, anymore. Boobs and a butt and a teensy tiny waist, and a mind long, long gone to liberal arts waste.

Two enforcers walked in, so modded out they were barely human.

In form, that is. Their minds and hearts were long gone. Never mind souls, if you believed in that sort of thing.

One, a tiger woman with lambent orange eyes, padded by on big furry clawed feet, claws click-clacking against the polished concrete floor. The tiger woman stared straight ahead, but her nose was twitching overtime, and those fuzzy ears twisted to listen to every tiny clink of tools. The other, a manic pixie girl dressed to the nines in a tight-bodiced, flare-skirted black vintage cocktail dress, sashayed next to her, her red metallic tendrils curling and swishing in the frigid stale air. Her green-eyed gaze bounced from worktable to conveyer belts and back again.

Enforcers. Maintenance Men, they called themselves. Checking the work. Checking for loyalty. Checking to make sure each one of *them*, the factory workers, exceeded their quotas. Sorting, picking, recovering. Rare metals, minerals, whatever value could be picked out of trash.

Never mind the bactosolvents penetrating your skin, doing who knows what to your DNA. The corneal scarring from the ever-present fumes. The low deep ache, punctuated by stabbing shocks, in your hands and forearms and your back that nothing, even SynFen, would relieve.

Betty had read the underground missives, the warnings, about the conditions at RecycleCity. Hard copy newsletters, left in the bathrooms, tucked into the toilet paper dispensers, left in between the stacked composite plates in the cafeteria. Read then crumbled the papers, flushing them or tossing them in the trash, too afraid to pass them along.

Because of the Maintenance Men.

The pixie girl dimpled at Betty, nodding at the filled trays in front of her. "Good job, babykins."

"Cute," murmured Betty, despite herself, and the red-haired, doll-like girl batted mink-thick eyelashes at her. Betty's first girlfriend back in college had been a petite green-eyed redhead.

"Back atchoo, skipperoo," the girl said, blowing her a kiss. "Keep up the super awesome work."

Her cherry red nails sparkled in the harsh fluorescent lights, moisture pooling at the tips. Who knew what poison coated those nails.

Those Maintenance Men were bug fuck crazy.

Betty had seen what they had done to one of the union guys, before *his* parts got recycled.

"Crip, trust me, you don't want to screw with your head," Betty muttered after they'd passed, her hands flying as she sorted through the pile of vintage ear buds, separating out the different plastics from the batteries, painting the plastic seams with bactosolvents til she could break them down to the smallest bits.

Her mama had died not knowing her daughters anymore. Mods gone awry, not Alzheimer's.

"Hands," he said, watching hers swiftly sort. "Maybe I'mma get me a new hand. Keep one hand human to keep the ladies happy, swap out t'other."

Betty was tired, but she was all *her*. One hundred percent human, no nanos, no mods, just her.

She could keep up with her quotas, enough to keep her fed and contribute to the roof over her head (her and three other roomies, hot bunking the beds, but still, air-controlled and weather-tight). Enough to put a little aside to maybe, just maybe, get her out of RecycleCity and into a better job, where she could really build up to something good. Something safer. Something *other*.

"Maybe get a new hand," Crip repeated. "With swappable fingertips."

"Still have to get a mod to use them," Betty said. "Take too long to get used to, otherwise. You'd never get caught back up." Bad things happened to people who didn't catch up. Parts and profits were worth more than whole people if you didn't stay on quota. She and her sisters were years, decades, chipping away at mama's debts.

"Baby, I'mma already modded, you jus' need to come over sometime after work and lemme show ya," he leered. "I can go all night. All day. All night. Dontcha worry about me."

She shoved her tray to the belt running down the center of the steel worktable, reached for another without realizing what was on it til it was in front of her, already noted on her account. Antique portable cassette players. Wow. She hadn't seen one of those since her daddy died and she was going through his hoard of belongings, including garbage from when he was just a boy. She'd thought they'd already be all gone by now. Someone found a cache. Raided a bombed-out junk store. Who knew.

Or maybe there was so little of worth in these pieces of junk that the tray kept circling until someone inattentive snagged it....she yanked on her vidglasses, tapped the earpiece.

"Value," she said, and the number that flashed nearly made her cry. She'd be in the hole after this, no matter how fast she worked.

And she couldn't put it back, grab another tray. It was already logged.

"What's wrong, sugar plum?"

A warm sweet vanilla breath tickled the back of Betty's neck. Sugar and spice and nothing, *nothing*, nice.

The little pixie Maintenance Man.

Bruce clenched the table's edge as the tiger woman grasped the back of his neck and then the tiger yanked, and dropped cervical vertebrae and tattered bloody meat and glistening spinal cord and lumpy medulla onto the empty tray in front of his lolling head, his startled sightless eyes staring straight at Betty, sitting across from him. Raawrr, the tiger said to Betty, and the doll-like girl smiled sweetly at Betty and said "Don't you worry, sugar plum, today's not your day."

"Nothing," Betty said. Abso-fucking-lutely nothing.

Crip sat stock still, precious seconds tick-tocking away. His titanium-tipped screwdriver snapped in his hand.

"Isn't that just awesome! You keep working, sugar plum." The girl swished away, high heels tip tapping.

"Jesus, Bets, you don' wanna mess with that one," Crip whispered. "She's worse than that tiger lady—"

"Woopsie!" the girl said, from two tables away, and a red tendril of metallic hair whipped at him, lengthening to reach him, to slice his weathered, wrinkled cheek like a piece of wet cardboard tearing. "If you don't have something nice to say, say it to my face!"

Blood dripped onto his tray, pooling around the tiny pile of batteries.

The tiger loped to them.

"Clean that up," the tiger growled, motioning to the tray. A tear from one rheumy eye dripped into the oozing cut on Crip's face as he dabbed the blood at his tray with the cuff of his sleeve. The nonabsorbent fiber just smeared the blood around.

She pointed one clawed finger at Betty.

"And you—*work*."

She turned to the pixie Maintenance Man.

"And, Kit-Kat, stop wasting their time. That's a ding against you, not just them, if they're under quota for today."

"They won't be. They don't dare, right, kiddos? Don't let me down, Buh-ruce!" She flounced away, the tiger woman stalking after her.

Betty fished a cotton bandanna, retro country turkey red and cream paisley, out of her personal bag. She usually used it to tied up her hair, but Crip needed it more. "Use this."

"I cain't miss quota," he said. "I was jus' talkin' big before, I ain't got no savings. No mods. Nothing for mods. Barely enough for food. I'm living at the coothole if I can't make rent in two days, and I don't think I will."

"Ka-*ching*!" called the girl.

How could she still hear them, all the other way across the floor, rows and rows of tables away, blast her perfect little face?

"Meet me at the corner company store and I'll buy you a mod so you can work like a boss!" the girl said. "No tricks, just a treat, just for you, old man! Just to say I'm sorry for slowing you down. Don't say Kit-Kat never did nothing for you."

The tiger growled.

"Don't, Crip," said Betty. "I'll help you." Somehow.

"Tick-tock, old man!"

"Sorry, Betty." He shoved his stool back from his station, eased himself down. "Comin', Miss Kit-Kat!" He limped to the two Maintenance Men, blood spattering the concrete floor in tiny drips. "Comin'!"

Betty reached for the first cassette player, letting her hair hid her face.

———

CRIP RETURNED TWO HOURS LATER, two hours til shift end. He didn't talk to her. Didn't look at her. His cheek was plastic-y smooth, and his yellow gray eyes glittered. His hands sped across his tray, arthritic knuckles popping and cracking, finishing it so fast that Betty's heart ached.

"Crip?" Betty said. "Crip, honey?"

"No one by that name," he said. "Advise avoidance."

"Oh, honey," she said. She finished her tray, her fifth since the cassette players, reached for another. Didn't say another word.

She wasn't crying. She wasn't.

It was just the fumes.

———

BETTY CLOCKED out at 7:12 p.m. She'd barely made quota, and waived payment for the extra twelve minutes.

She didn't know anyone who'd ever accepted overtime. Bruce had argued they should. And look what happened to him.

Crip still sat at his station when she left, methodically breaking down vintage wrist-worn fitness trackers. Far as she knew, he'd be staying all night.

Fifteen minutes to walk home through the air-controlled tunnel system. A little longer than walking topside, but worth it.

Ten minutes to trudge up the stairs to her twentieth floor apartment. The elevator broke down three years ago. Two people died when it splatted in the basement. The elevator got fixed, but Betty had never trusted it.

Five minutes to dig through the shared fridge, find her batch of almost-expired, discounted nutripacks. One pack was missing. Probably Danielle took it. Betty couldn't care. Too tired. Too heartsick.

Two minutes to heat it up, three to force it down, then one to stagger to the lower bunk she swapped with Carrie. Melissa snored softly in the top bunk.

And one more to fall asleep, promising herself tomorrow would be different. Somehow.

——————

SHE WOKE to the smell of coffee. Coffee! She hadn't had real coffee for thirty years, but that smell...that rich, bitter, warm smell...it zinged against her nose and her brain and got her mouth watering. Didn't matter that no light penetrated the triple-paned plexi, the news scroll across the bottom was halted, and the house wake-up ringer was silent, it was time to get up.

She pulled on a gray work top, buttoned it with shaking fingers. Yanked on faux-cotton jeans. Slid her feet into her worn black flats, base fibers showing through the scuffed pleather.

"Hiya, sugar plum!"

That Maintenance Man Kit-Kat sat at their chipped granite countertop, back straight, legs daintily crossed at the ankle. She wore a sleeveless velvet sheath and big glossy pearls around her neck. Her feet were bare, the bottoms soiled; her high heeled sandals dangled from one small hand. Her cherry red lipstick was fuzzy along her lower lip, and her sooty lashes had bled under her eyes.

"I like you," Kit-Kat said. "Spunky. Cute. You need a tune up, but hey! I know a guy."

She smiled, her green eyes bright against her smudged mascara.

"I was up *all night* thinking about you. And I think I got an offer for you. You know, that you can't—"

"I got it," Betty said shortly. She could smell something else. Metallic. Meat.

"Coffee?" Kit-Kat slipped off the stool, walked ballerina-straight to the back kitchen counter. "Bought you a French press. Like it?"

Kit-Kat poured a mug of coffee, handed it to Betty, who took it, willing her hands steady.

"Sorry, forgot to get sugar or cream. I can buy those, you know," she added. "I can buy all sorts of creature comforts."

"Where are my roommates?" Betty whispered. *Meat*.

"Well, Sweet Caroline was still at RecycleCity when I headed over. I convinced the rest to leave us alone for a bit." She hopped back up on the worn pleather-cushioned stool. "Or something that amounts to that. So! Just the two of us. Alone together at last, sugar plum."

Kit-Kat leaned forward, elbows on the counter, chin resting on steepled hands. She lowered her lashes, looked up coyly. Batted her lashes.

Betty sipped the coffee. It tasted bitter and flat, burnt rubber skids along a potholed road. It tasted like dead roommates. If she could get Kit-Kat to leave before Carrie got home, maybe she could at least keep Carrie safe.

"See! That sense of loyalty. I can see it in your eyes, feel it in my heart. You don't care about yourself, just that sad old man and your waste-of-resources pals."

"Leave them out of this."

"Well, that old man is now having the time of his life. Worked all night! He loved you, you know. Sort of like a daughter but wow, that means those daydreams he's living in are a little incestuous! And your roomies....well. It wasn't much of a life, anyways, for them, right, babykins? Sweet Caroline....she'll be home in what, twenty minutes? She still has her sad desperate dead-end life.

"But you...I think you have potential. Great potential. If you're willing to step up and grab it. The natives are restless. Your Bruce wasn't alone. Misguided souls. But still, growing in number. We can read, too.

"We could use a gal like you, sugar plum. PinUp Betty, Maintenance Man extraordinaire! Hair to here, boobs to there! Can't you see it? See yourself?"

"Never."

Kit-Kat pouted. "Sugar plum, don't let me down. And I'm giving you a choice."

"Not really." Betty was tired. So tired. "If you want to change me, you will."

"Well, yes. But it's ever so much better if you say yes. If you choose." Kit-Kat sat up, took the half-full cup of coffee from Betty, then grasped her hands.

Her hands were hot, red hot, against Betty's cold skin. So cold. Betty felt like she was already gone. Like Crip. Danielle. Melissa.

Caroline was still out there. Fifteen minutes from home.

From death.

"Okay," Betty said.

"Oh, goodie! Come on, come on! I'll take you to the company lab. It's ever so clean and modern. We'll get you in tip-top shape. How old am I do you think? Tell the truth!"

"You look early twenties."

"Forty-three! I'm forty-three." She cocked her head. "I know you're fifty-two. A very well preserved fifty-two, despite working ten years at RecycleCity. We'll have you at twenty-nine forever!"

"I walk a lot," Betty said. "I take the stairs, instead of the elevator."

"That does seem really rickety, doesn't it?"

"I don't trust it. Can we go down the stairs instead?"

"Sure thing, sugar plum!"

Betty pulled the door shut behind them. Locked it, thumb pressed against the ancient reader. Looked over the stair rail. Twenty floors straight down.

She heard the click of the entryway door, twenty floors down. Carrie.

One chance. One last choice that was hers.

Betty dove headfirst over the rail.

Kit-Kat's lethal hair stretched for her, sliced the legs of her faux cotton jeans, sliced the skin underneath.

Betty fell in a shower of blood. Heard Carrie's scream, right before—

Didn't matter. She was done.

———————————

"Hey guys! I'm heading to corporate, so I want to introduce my replacement! She hurt herself, but we got her all fixed up!

"Isn't she just a doll, a pin-up doll? Meet PinUp Betty. That gorgeous blond hair all the way to here, and those magnificent boobs all the way out to there! She'll be working with Jeanie, that big ole scary tiger, to keep you all on the straight and narrow!"

Kit-Kat sashayed down each row of tables, tugging Betty along, Betty in a red halter top and white capris and thick blonde hair bundled back by a turkey red paisley bandanna. Jeanie the tiger woman stalked behind them, grumbling.

"Say hi to your old friend Crip, Betty!"

"Hi, you handsome hunk of seasoned manhood. How's the work going?"

"Going fine, Miss Betty! Say, haven't we met before?"

"Don't you think I'd remember *you*? I could never, ever forget a man like you," Pin Up Betty purred. "Never, never, never!"

OF PARROTS AND PIGEONS

CASEY GRIPPED THE VERTICAL SECURITY BAR AS THE BLUE GARBAGE truck rumbled up 3rd Street, shifting to keep her balance. Her hands were sweaty in her thick leather gloves. Carlos, her driver, stopped every few houses for Casey to jump off and pull the blue bins into position so the hydraulic container arm could grab and dump each one.

By the end of her eight hour shift, her knees would be creaking and her shoulders miserably tight. On top of being all sweaty and stinky. And exhausted in general.

Didn't help there'd been a quake centered on Hawthorne, just a few miles away, last night, that had wakened her. 5.3. Big enough for even a native Californian to take note.

Only thirty-three and she felt like fifty years old.

Some crews swapped driving and loading, but Carlos had lost both legs below the knees in Iran and the state-supplied prosthetics were lowest bidder. She'd seen him at the end of a run, blood staining the bandages around his stumps, and quietly insisted he drive from there on. He didn't like it, but the chance of antibiotic resistant secondary infections, and the economic impact of unpaid sick time, made him acquiesce.

They were on the recycling run today. Lots of heavy wine bottles, lots of craft beer cans with bright labels. Stacks of expensive glossy paper magazines (who got those, still? apparently lots of rich folks here in the Beach Cities, south of Los Angeles International Airport, people who could afford them and just toss them). And stained greasy pizza boxes, ubiquitous to every neighborhood she'd collected in, that would be sorted into trash at the recycling center, because darn it, dirty paper was not recyclable.

Casey was overdressed for the sticky weather, but appropriate for the job, long sleeved shirt with sleeves buttoned at the wrist; orange and yellow mesh security vest; sturdy cotton khakis; and leather work boots to match the heavy gloves. Her long black hair was tied up in a high ponytail, but tendrils escaped to stick against her neck and forehead.

Everything would smell, like sour wine and stale beer and her own sweat, but not as bad as the regular trash days. Even washing the clothes twice and her hair three times she'd still stink on *those* days.

Of course once in a while some asshole put a fragrant dog poop bag into the recycling bins.

That sucked.

Sucked, too, that, even with a master's in ornithology and a teaching certificate, Casey had to supplement her income with working as a garbage collector. She taught part time distance learning for the community college, Bio 101 and Environmental Sciences, in the late afternoon til early evening. Yay for today's economy.

At least she was working. And at least she got to be outside, even if it was too hot and too humid and the air quality indicators were stuck at hazardous.

At least she got to watch for the wild parrots.

She'd started collecting data on the feral parrots that nested in colonies in the palm trees, usually unseen but definitely, oh most definitely, *heard*. Her own private project. She missed field research, those summer months she'd spent in Costa Rica studying scarlet macaws. This was a pale imitation, but she had to do *something*.

The parrots, along with the coyotes and crows and raccoons, were thriving in the South Bay Beach Cities of Los Angeles: Manhattan, Hermosa, and Redondo. But the latter species belonged here—or at least their habitat under laid all the concrete and asphalt. The parrots had moved in. She respected that, their resilience. Escapees, torn away from their original homes, the parrots were doing the best they could.

Casey was always amazed that something so big and green could hide so well, once they were settled in the trees.

She squinted through her sunglasses. Even with the haze of pollution, the sunlight was bright.

The house at the top of the street had a big fig tree in their front yard, that a murder of crows had claimed as theirs. But last week she'd seen a half dozen parrots flocking towards it, now that the overripe fruit was splatting against the sidewalk, perfuming the air with fermented sweetness. The parrots might be there again, feasting. They weren't afraid of the crows, especially when they outnumbered the crows.

Bright green winged towards the fig tree.

Four different species of parrots—well, parakeets—were commonly found in Hermosa Beach: Mitred and Red-masked, both with red on their faces, and White-winged and Yellow-chevroned, with green heads. They weren't like the tiny blue or pale yellow pet store parakeets, or budgies. They looked like parrots.

This parrot had an orange, not red, face, and a bright yellow head.

No parrot in the Los Angeles area looked like that, let alone the ones common to the Beach Cities.

A second, then a third, and then a fourth joined the first on the fig tree.

Casey glanced up at the electrical wires running overhead and gasped.

"Stop the truck!" She banged on the ash-streaked passenger side window. Carlos, startled, braked. Clinging to the vertical pole with one hand, one foot slipping on the textured running board, Casey yanked her phone out of her pocket to get a picture.

Heart pounding, she juggled her phone one handed, gave up, and jumped off the running board. She stumbled, the ground quivering underfoot. Aftershock. She took a dozen pictures and a video to boot, shifting her weight to maintain her balance.

At least fifty parrots with yellow heads and orange faces looked back down at her. Maybe more, as she scanned other nearby wires, the wires sagging with the weight of all the birds.

These parrots were big, bigger than the regular local parakeets, by a good four inches head to tail. They were chattering amongst themselves, their voices raspy. One more flew down to the fig tree, showing off its nearly two-foot wingspan.

She uploaded the best photo to her birding app, fingers trembling.

But she knew what it was going to say.

She *knew* parrots.

Her heart skipped at the all-caps EXTINCT label, flashing across the top of the entry that popped up.

The Carolina Parakeet, *Conuropsis carolinensis*.

The only native North American parrot, extinct for over a hundred years.

Not extinct, despite the flashing banner.

Here. *Now*.

The parakeets all launched themselves from the wires, a cloud large enough to blot out the sun and cast shade on the ground.

———

THEY HAD to finish their route. Even if Casey hadn't needed the job, even if she could just quit and spend the rest of her days watching those gorgeous green parrots, she could never have left Carlos hanging.

And everywhere she looked, as they drove up and down the streets and she jumped off and on to position and move bins, she saw more and more Carolina Parakeets. Squawking and chattering, their dark brown eyes alight, they explored the neighborhood as the garbage truck trundled along. They seemed curious, more than wary, of the truck and other vehicles.

And there were enough of them they were messy. As bad as the seagulls, except there were, by this time, close to the end of her shift, far more parrots than gulls, at least in the neighborhood. The stink of fruity guano plopping along the sidewalks and streets and cars, more than the beat of wings that cooled her face and the chuckling chatter that filled her ears, made her believe the parakeets were truly there.

That it wasn't just the despair of the last few years finally cracking her mind.

"What are you going to do the rest of the day, chica?" Carlos asked when they finally reached the depot in Gardena, emptied the truck, and parked it.

Carolina Parakeets!

"I'm going to text my thesis advisor Dr Forst," Casey said. Dr Anna Forst, an ornithologist at Cal State San Diego, loved parrots as much as Casey did. Only ten years older than Casey, Anna was as much big sister as professor. "Then...I don't know. Back to Hermosa, I guess, to start counting. And recording. You?"

He smiled. "Gonna get my kids and take them to El Dorado Park in Long Beach. Show them the birds. This is something else, eh, Casey? Hope, maybe. Maybe something good is happening."

She nodded. Maybe not everything in the world was ruined. Maybe there was hope.

A flash of grayish turquoise blue, way bigger than the parakeets, caught her eye, and she held her breath. *Anodorhynchus glaucus*. Why not? The Glaucous macaw was considered most likely extinct, unlike the Carolina Parakeet, which was *definitely* extinct.

Well, at least til now. Her heart soared with the large blue macaw.

It made just as much sense to see a Glaucous Macaw as it did Carolina Parakeets. And shoot, none of these birds had *ever* lived in California.

If she travelled up into the mountains, would she see California grizzlies? Southern California Kit Foxes on her drive there, through the desert leading to the peaks? Tecopa pupfish in desert hot springs, if she stopped for a soak?

Or was it just birds, returning?

What to say to Anna that wouldn't sound crazy?

Hi! Hope u r doing well. Casey paused, then hit send.

R they there too?

Noncommittal. But if the same thing was happening in San Diego, it would make sense to Anna.

Casey got into her old dinged up Prius, swapped out her boots for sneakers, and drove back the seven and a half miles back to Hermosa.

She pulled in to the last spot on the top level of the parking structure near the pier.

It was like night and day, the amount of wealth in real estate in Hermosa, compared to Gardena; but flocks of parakeets filled the electrical wires and palms in Gardena just as much as in the beach town.

The birds didn't know or care.

But she loved the ocean almost as much as she loved parrots. And if she could be by both at once, well, she couldn't think of anything better.

The pier area was packed with both people, gawking at the birds, and parrots and macaws, shrieking back at them from the tall palms lining what used to be the end of Pier Avenue until it was converted to pedestrian only, years ago.

Long-tailed, rose-breasted pigeons mingled with the regular smaller sturdy gray city pigeons.

At this point, even passenger pigeons didn't surprise Casey. Maybe if an American lion or a saber-toothed tiger or a dire wolf came trotting down the street, something out of the tar pits made flesh....

Her phone vibrated.

Call me!!!!

Anna.

Casey hit call as she dodged people walking out onto the pier. A half dozen large seals were hauled out on the wet sand below, dark eyes glinting in the sunlight. She didn't know pinnipeds like she knew parrots, but they weren't sea lions, or harbor seals. And definitely not elephant seals, not even female elephant seals, who lacked the large proboscis of the males.

Tiny porpoises surfed the waves as she walked further out.

Anna answered.

"Casey? Oh my god, I can't believe this—"

"Carolina Parakeets, Glaucous Macaws, and passenger pigeons. Some weird seal on the beach, and I think vaquitas are in the water," Casey said.

"Yes! Monk seals, by the way. Caribbean Monk Seals. I don't know how they'd ended up here, the water is too cold for them, but...they were here for just an hour or so, then started swimming north. The birds left just a little later. I have some students driving up the coast, tracking them as best they can."

Casey leaned against the rough unpainted railing, avoiding seagull splotches. The seals caterpillared their way into the surf as she watched and began swimming south. The school of vaquitas followed.

With a rush of wings, audible even from as far out as she was on the pier, the macaws and parrots and pigeons flew up, then sped south as well.

"They're leaving here, too," Casey said. "They just got here, and they're leaving." She wiped at her eyes. It the sun, damn it, just the sunlight and pollution causing her to cry.

"North or south, Casey?"

"South."

"Follow them."

"Okay. I'll call you when I find out anything." Casey took a deep breath, then started jogging to her car.

She could see huge flocks of birds overhead, green and blue and gray, all heading south towards the Palos Verdes Peninsula. The western side of Palos Verdes, or PV, was a mix of expensive homes and rough cliffs and hillsides. Tide pools dotted the coast. There had been a fancy resort right on the edge of the peninsula, but rising waters and worsening storms had turned it into a ghost town of abandoned buildings. Beyond that, past the geologically unstable ground of Portuguese Bend, fit only for hiking when the air quality allowed, the Trump National Golf Course had slid into the ocean.

She drove along Pacific Coast Highway to Palos Verdes Drive West, windows open so she could hear the squawks of the parrots. The birds, all land birds, stayed overhead, their flight path following the road, not venturing over the water. Past the old resort, past the roller-coaster roads of Portuguese Bend, and just past the slumped bluffs of the golf course.

The birds were circling over White Point Park. She parked and jogged to the beach, holding her phone up, recording as much as she could. A glistening, translucent wall rose up from the golden sandy beach, and cut over the tidepools and over the ocean. The vaquitas were leaping into the air and through the wall; monk seals were swimming through it.

And the parrots and macaws and pigeons were flying through it.

"No, no, no," Casey said. As each creature flew or swam or leaped through the wall—wall? curtain? barrier?, light pulsed. And though Casey could see something—bright blue sky instead of orange-tinted fog—through the barrier, and the animals themselves—she could tell they were passing from her world.

Back to theirs.

The ground shifted under her feet.

The parrots screamed, divebombing past Casey, flinging themselves at the barrier.

Casey lurched as the ground bucked and shuddered. The ocean was receding, exposing slick green algae and olive colored kelp on the nearby rocks. Casey stumbled after the water, trying to get to the barrier. A small orange octopus, stranded in the closest tide pool, darted frantically back and forth. She couldn't help the octopus.

She couldn't help *anything*.

The barrier flickered, shining waves of iridescence illuminating the beach. The ocean had pulled back ten, twenty yards, and Casey's feet found purchase on the sloping hardpacked wet sand.

The ocean would return, those twenty yards and more, and at the back of her mind Casey knew she was risking death.

But she had to *see*. See where the vaquitas and seals swam, see where the birds flew.

Other birds flew past her. Native seagulls and kestrels, and her small feral parrots, Mitred and Red-masked, White-winged and Yellow-chevroned. Sea lions bellowed and followed the monk seals. Bottlenose dolphins, still swimming in deep enough water, joined their little cousins.

All through the barrier. Swimming or flying like their lives depended on it.

Casey's phone vibrated. Anna.

"I found it!" Casey gasped, still running. Anna said something back. Casey couldn't understand her. The birds, the sea lions, even the churning rumble of the ground, still moving, filled her head.

"I can't hear you!" Casey said, then hit end. She paused and took a picture of the barrier, just a few yards ahead of her now, and messaged it to Anna.

A late afternoon sun blazed in a brilliant blue sky, just beyond the barrier. Casey tasted brine, sharp and clean, on her tongue. A brisk salty wind cooled her sweaty face.

And a woman, matching Casey's height and build, dressed in an indigo simple shift, held out her hand to Casey.

Hope.

I have 2 go, Casey texted Anna. *Sorry*.

Sorry, Carlos. Sorry, students.

Casey stepped through the barrier.

THE DEATH OF INNOCENTS

SELENE SINGH WRIGGLED INTO HER REPRO VINTAGE PLEATHER jumpsuit, ignoring the bittersweet sigh from the so-lovely, so-muscled, so-forgettable man lounging on her travel room's narrow bunk.

The travel rooms allotted to economy passengers on the planet jumper class ship *Questing Beast* were spartan, with just enough room for a one-person, two meter long bunk with storage underneath; a desktop, made of a cream-colored honeycombed, lightweight ceramic material, that pulled down from the wall and settled over the bunk; and a folding chair seat of similar material that pulled down from the wall opposite. A wall screen occupied the wall opposite the door. The rest of the walls were unadorned, just the molded, dingy off-white walls that filled the lower class passenger areas of the ship. Dirt wedged in the junction between the dark gray rubberized floor and the walls.

Communal ultrasonic showers were down the narrow hallway just outside, as was a credit-operated kitchenette for when passengers wanted to eat in the privacy of their rooms.

The air smelled stale and antiseptic after two days of travel, with an overlay of sex from her recent activities.

She couldn't wait to finish her mission and get off this ship.

Selene had chosen *dark side moonscape* rather than a newsfeed or planetary landscape for the wall screen. She would have preferred simply switching the screen to transparent, and looking out into space, but only the higher decks rated the more expensive transparent screens.

The dark expanse settled her mind. Helped her ignore the tiny quarters, the dead air.

It *was* better than steerage class. At least in economy, you got your own room to yourself.

Unless you wanted company. Something to pass the time.

He took up most of the space on the thin firm mattress, the sheet draped artfully over his pale blue narrow pelvis.

His people had tweaked their genes so that their skin would reflect their moods. Blue was sad, lavender aroused, pink happy. Basic.

But colorful. Pretty, if you didn't mind that asphyxiated look. His posing and pouting had been tolerable earlier, when he focused on providing a performance for her. He was a low rent vid model, and she suspected he sold himself as well as his looks to keep that physique steroid-pumped.

Regardless, he hadn't charged her for his services.

But now, she had a job to do.

"Sorry, lover, I have to go," Selene said as she zipped up the front of her suit. The matte black fabric followed the curves and muscles of her petite figure. She stepped into her rubber-soled leather boots and buckled them.

If someone could look past her fine-featured face, with her golden eyes, high cheekbones, and tawny, sunlight-kissed skin; her straight blue-black hair, pulled back into a ponytail of thin braids; her soft musical voice...they might realize just how lethal she was. Might realize that the popular retro jumpsuit was highly customized, with various weapons, cloakers, and field disruptors tucked into discreet pockets. And explosives, enough to destroy the *Questing Beast*, lined the seams.

Might look past the warm eyes to the blankness behind them.

But no one ever did. Certainly not the man on the bunk. And she was fine with that.

"But, Sella, do you really have to leave now?" he said.

"Sorry, lover, I do." She'd forgotten his name. "You were wonderful. But shoo. Out." She smiled sweetly.

He stood up and stretched, showing off his finely muscled body, ignoring the sheet slipping off, baring every glorious inch.

She tossed his trousers and tank top to him, laughing. "Out."

He dressed quickly, then, and left. She stopped laughing as soon as she pushed the button that slide the door shut. She gave him sixty seconds.

Then left the room.

————

HER TARGET, Count Christopher St Alcene, heir to the St Alcene pan-planetary corporation Worldseekers, traveled in Galaxy Class. Her organization, Galactic Intel Collective, or GIC, had offered to book her into first, one deck below, but Selene noted that her cover, Sella Woo, tabloid journalist from *News This Week*, would barely be able to charge economy to her business account.

People paid more attention to first class travelers.

She didn't want attention, at least not the sort the upper class travelers created. She'd taken two days to establish herself as Sella Woo: perky, ambitious, sexy Sella.

"St Alcene had been a bad, bad boy," her handler, Richard Lane, told her during her last briefing. Lane was the nephew of her last handler, Damien Krause. She would never admit it to Damien, and barely admitted it to herself, but by the time Damien had retired, he was more than a handler: he'd become a surrogate father to her.

"Richie is a good kid," Damien had told her *"He'd had some issues at University, but he's grown up since then. Be patient with him."*

"Half a dozen cover ups, drugs, trafficking, that we've dug up," Lane had continued. "But what interests GIC, and what needs to stop, are his clandestine military sales."

Selene didn't care about any of cover ups. You do you.

But she did care about fulfilling her mission: to make sure, by any and all means necessary, that St Alcene wouldn't continue selling combat-modified ships to the highest bidder. To *any* bidder.

And *couldn't* was just as acceptable as *wouldn't*. Easier, in fact.

She passed the communal kitchenette, then took the elevator at the end of the narrow hallway to the entertainment deck.

The entertainment deck was misnamed; it only occupied two thirds of the fourth deck, the rest being dedicated to storage. But, on a ship this size, it was the only area allotted for recreation.

A bar offered various inebriatory chemicals. A long dull metal topped the counter, upholstered barstools crowded up to it, and smaller tables in dark corners offered more private seating. A small contained first and galaxy class dining area, with actual windows that she could just see through the doorway, was opposite the bar. A larger dining area for economy and steerage behind her. A gym, for those who gained their fitness the old-fashioned way, was adjacent to the economy dining area. A gambling room, tucked beyond the bar, included various gambling tables, passengers already hard at work losing money.

The scent of the eucalyptus shower gel from the gym overrode the recyled air staleness. She'd have to remember it, if she wanted to have an actual shower with water, not just the ultrasonic.

Ah...as she expected, from all the reports of debauchery. St Alcene sat at the far end of the zinc-topped bar, his attention on the squat android barkeep currently mixing a drink.

An older man, dressed in neat pleathers like her jumpsuit, with a visible blaster, sat at the nearest end. St Alcene's bodyguard, she was sure.

If her momentary dalliance (what *was* his name?) was pretty, St Alcene was in a different class altogether. The images in his dossier didn't really capture him his stunning appearance. His skin was dark and smooth, his features narrow and intense. The vibrancy in his taut body gave her an uneasy chill.

This didn't seem like the vacuous party boy the dossier discussed.

Didn't matter.

She slipped onto the upholstered stool next to his. "Rye Manhattan," she said. "Up, two cherries."

St Alcene glanced at her. "Old school," he said, his voice a rich baritone.

She shrugged. "A girl's gotta drink what she loves to drink."

"Christopher," he said, holding out his hand.

"Sella. Journalist for the *News This Week*."

"Ah," he said, pulling his hand back.

"You'd've found out in less than a minute, anyways," she said, eyes flicking to the small comms piece in his left ear. "I'm sure that nice bodyguard of yours at the far end of the bar is telling you right now."

She caught the outraged stiffening of the bodyguard's stance out of the corner of her eye. Sloppy. If he were hers, she'd fire him.

St Alcene smiled tightly. "You're perceptive."

"It's my job." She leaned towards him, touched his sleeve. Real silk, not synth, the rich navy fabric cool against her skin. "But I need to take a break from work."

"Sel!"

Selene turned.

The blue boy, his wide violet eyes betrayed, stood a couple feet away. He wore a sheer cotton tunic, showing off the deep distressed blue of his chiseled torso, and loose fitting black cotton pants hanging off his hip bones.

"I thought you said you had things to do," he said, his cheekbones blotchy navy.

"I do," she said. "Better things than you."

"I think you're busy enough right now, Miss Woo," St Alcene said, arching an elegant eyebrow, examining the blue boy like he himself might be interested. "Perhaps I'll see you later." He stood, motioned to his bodyguard, and left.

Well, at least her cover as Sella was holding.

————

IT HAD TAKEN her cruel words, and finally, a threat of a restrictive perimeter, to get rid of the boy.

There was no way she could offer St Alcene anything to make him stop. She'd realized that as soon as she sat next to him. Money wouldn't matter. Power might, but she had none to offer him, and she now, despite the briefing, knew he was the sort of man would want to *take* power, not be given it.

Removal it was, then. And afterwards, when she completed her mission brief, a recommendation of censure for whoever put together that dossier.

She couldn't enjoy her beverage, the spicy rye, the sweetness of the cherries. But Sella Woo couldn't afford to waste a pricy drink, so she drank it slowly, watching as more passengers filtered into the various areas of the entertainment deck. It was near dinnertime, shiptime. She ordered a small meal, protobeef loaf that tasted three days too old, with braised bitter greens, overcooked into a soft soggy mess, then a second drink to wash down the food.

And then watched, an hour later, as St Alcene entered the Galaxy class dining room, bodyguard in tow.

Time for Plan B. She finished her drink and the last scraps of her meal, thanked the android barkeep, then left.

———

THE *QUESTING BEAST*'s livery varied little from other ships. Selene programmed one of her cloakers with the differences, then activated it. To casual observation, she looked like one of the androids in charge of cleaning rooms and restocking supplies: ship's uniform, smooth pale androgynous face, bald head. Good enough to get her to the Galaxy class deck, top of the ship, without anyone noticing her.

No one looked at androids.

The Galaxy class deck contained six suites. She'd studied the layout of the ship before boarding. St Alcene had booked two of the six, both along the starboard side of the ship. If she could confirm he was alone in either of them, she could seal the vents and poison the cabin air.

Or even if he wasn't alone.

But she preferred not to take the lives of other people just doing their jobs. St Alcene's servants didn't deserved to be murdered.

And anyways, poison wasn't foolproof, and she was leery of doing anything that would tip him off.

Best to infiltrate, wait til he was alone, and just complete the mission quietly and efficiently.

She used a scanner to assess the occupancy of each suite. The right suite was empty. The other suite had someone lying on the bed.

None of the other suites on deck were occupied.

Her packet had included an employee pass-cuff to the Galaxy deck suites. She held her wrist up to the laser scanner of the rightmost suite. It obligingly chimed. The door slid open.

As expected, the first suite was empty. She barely registered the floor to ceiling window screens, switched to transparent to show the darkness of space, stars like glittering jewels against the velvety blackness. The air was fresh and cool. The doorway had opened into the living area, with a plush upholstered sectional in the center, the fabric a muted olive green. Copper end tables flanked either side. A small kitchenette and bar, open to the living room, was to the left.

Underfoot was a thick carpet, luxurious compared to the standard rubber floors. Her boots sunk into it.

The bedroom and adjoining bathroom was to her right. She peeked in. No one there.

The suites were connected by a closed doorway. She held up her pass-cuff, and it opened. The living area mirrored that of the first suite, with a royal blue sectional.

It was quiet, quiet as the first suite.

But it didn't smell as fresh.

A metallic tang. A whiff of feces. Stronger as she approached the bedroom.

"Oh, no," she said, standing at the doorway into the bedroom.

Blue boy lay flat on the bed, nude, muscled arms and legs spread wide. His lovely violet eyes, pupils dilated, stared at nothing. His throat was sliced, soaking the white silk coverlet beneath him with dark red blood.

She barely registered the hiss of the suite door opening behind her.

"He didn't tell me anything about you," St Alcene said from behind her. "I do think he truly knew nothing. That he believed you were a young woman named Sella Woo, on assignment from *News This Week*."

"My name *is* Sella Woo," she said, turning to him. "And I am a journalist. And I've just stumbled onto the biggest story of my life. A murdering playboy heir."

"Really, Selene? Agent 696 of the GIC?"

Blown.

This mission stank of deceit and lies.

"You didn't have to kill him," Selene said.

"Oh, please, don't tell me you actually care." St Alcene walked past her to the sectional, overhead lights brightening as he gestured to them. He sat on the sectional, facing the window screen. He patted the cushion. "Uncloak yourself. Sit. I'm sure we can come to some sort of accommodation."

"I don't want to die," she said, sitting kitty-corner to him, deactivating the cloaker. "So I'll listen."

He eyed her appreciatively. He saw what she wanted him to see: a beautiful, frightened, mercenary spy.

He didn't look past the fear in her eyes to the blankness behind it.

"Your untimely demise can be stalled, if you agree to work for me as well as GIC."

"How can I trust you?"

"You don't have a choice, Selene."

"They'll know something went wrong, if you continue selling gunships."

"Make something up. You excel at that, correct?"

She stared at him silently. Then reached out, stroked his hand. "You leave me no choice."

———

He hadn't trusted her, making her remove her jumpsuit and boots before he let her any closer. Smart of him.

An hour later she left the suite. She'd borrowed one of the ship's robes from the bathroom. She still wore the pass-cuff.

She left the jumpsuit crumpled on the thick carpet of the living room floor. Discarded. Forgotten.

By him, if not by her. Maybe not so clever. Or maybe just complacent in his power.

The air of the corridor was recycled. Sour. But she welcomed it, over the cold purity of the air in the suite. The coldness of the silk coverlet, in the first bedroom. The chill wrapped around her heart.

Jay. The boy's name was Jay de Ranoi.

She'd finally remembered.

She rode the elevator down to the Economy Class level. She held the pass-cuff up to the scanner after she exited. "Note catastrophic hull breach, sensors disabled, Suite 1B. Seal top deck."

The scanner chimed in response.

She continued to her room. Dug out the transmitter to her jumpsuit. And detonated the explosives that filled the seams of the suit.

THE *QUESTING BEAST* hobbled to the closest port. The Galaxy Class deck was completely destroyed. Count Christopher St Alcene, the only occupant of the deck at the time, was declared dead, though no remains were recovered.

No one cared about Jay de Ranoi. He was declared missing, likely dead, though no one knew how he would've ended up on the Galaxy Class deck.

Selene leased a one-person shuttle back to GIC headquarters, a three day solo journey.

It gave her three days to think.

Three days to try to figure out who betrayed her, who didn't want the mission to succeed.

Three days to figure out who underestimated her.

She patched through to her independent sources. Three days was time for a lot of digging, when you had access to hackers like she did.

Follow the money, she ordered. Follow it, wherever it goes.

As she piloted into the agency dock and landed her shuttle, all the answers flooded in over her internal net.

Follow the money. And it all led back to Richard Lane.

Richard, who'd been her handler the past two years. Who'd come from a family with long term Agency members. The nephew of the man she considered a father.

Who'd given her no reason not to trust him.

Had she missed something? Been too complacent, trusted too much in her love for his uncle?

She logged the shuttle in with the on duty desk jockey monitoring the dock from his glassed-in office overlooking the dock and all the incoming and outgoing traffic. "Don't return it yet," she asked.

"Sure thing," he replied. "Need it cleaned out and restocked?"

She considered. "I'm not sure. So that's a yes. Priority on that?"

"Can do."

"Thanks." She left the dock office.

A tram ride later, she exited at GIC headquarters. The sunlight felt alien against her skin, even after less than a week away. The air was too fresh, too vegetal, as she walked across the plaza from the tram stop to the main entrance. The grass had been clipped recently, shorn to a velvety nub.

The building, a large y-shaped concrete block when viewed from above, each wing with bands of glass windows denoting each floor, was even bigger underground than it was above. GIC kept its secrets buried.

What if this went beyond Lane? She trusted her sources, but no one was perfect.

It didn't matter. She had to confront Lane. That's what she controlled, right now.

"Agent Singh, reporting in to debrief her mission," she told the guard, Frank, a older man who'd worked the guard desk longer than she'd been an agent. Rumor had it he'd served as a field agent, decades ago. One of the best. He eyed her jumpsuit, a duplicate of the one she'd used to blow up the Galaxy Class deck, warily.

He knew what kind of clothing and toys GIC created for its agents. Heck, what kind of equipment he'd likely had. And what was allowed at headquarters, even when worn by trusted agents.

"Frank, I just got here from the dock. Didn't even go home. Just let me report, okay? Richard's in, right?"

"Hasn't left his office all morning," Frank confirmed. He knew she didn't need anything other than her hands and feet to wreak havoc.

"Head up now, you'll catch him before lunch. Go on, before I change my mind."

She took the glass-walled elevator up to the 30th floor. Lane's office was at the end of one wing, with a view of the milky glacial waters of Lake Eliza.

He looked up from his terminal and blanched when she walked through his door and shut the door behind her. She pulled a disrupter from one of the many pockets on her jumpsuit, and activated it. No one could monitor anything inside the officer until she deactivated it.

She sat it atop his desk. She didn't need to slam it down. He knew what it was, and what it meant.

Younger than her by a dozen years, he was short, barely taller than her, and thin and nervous, with close-cropped brown hair already silvering at the temples. Sweat trickled down his forehead.

"Hands flat on the desk. Don't even think of calling for help,"

"I—"

"You set me up."

"I—"

"That sociopath murdered a boy, just to try to scare me.

"And then I. Blew. Him. Up." She walked around the desk, behind him. He smelled sour.

"Tell me why I shouldn't do the same to you."

"I—"

"I, I, I. That tells me nothing. Tick tock, Lane." She thought of Jay. Leaned in. Breathed on the back of his neck. "Tick tock."

"If I tell you, they'll kill me."

"Lane, you know my response to that."

He shook his head.

She sighed. *Jay*. Reached for the garrote tucked into the wrist seam of this jumpsuit.

"Was it just you?"

His knuckles whitened.

"Even if you don't tell me, I'll find out."

"Can't," he whispered.

She considered. Glanced at the framed vid on his desk. Two little boys, young, not more than five or six, waving. A wife, pretty, beaming, standing behind the kids.

She couldn't threaten his family.

She didn't want to think of what this would do to Damien.

Take care of this problem. She could hunt down the others later.

"I understand. It sucks when people involve innocents." *Jay*. She looped the thin wire around his neck and yanked.

SHE LEFT HQ, nodding at Frank on her way out. "I didn't do anything you wouldn't have done," she said.

But she didn't stop to explain herself to him.

She'd left a thumb drive including all the data her sources had sent. Including her report of the events on the *Questing Beast*.

She was in a hurry. She had a mission to complete. A mission of her own.

THE MERMAID OF ELLIS PRIME

KILLAINE LOUNGED IN THE WEB OF THE THICK, CROOKED BRANCHES of the mangrove tree, back against the rough barked trunk, long legs stretched out in front of her. Her sandals, the straps woven from a native linen-like material, hung off the tip of a nearby branch. Sticky golden sap peppered her narrow bare feet.

She could see just a hint of pale, cloudless blue sky between the soft feathery moss festooning the rough bark of the branches arching overhead. A breeze, redolent with a light jasmine scent, relieved some of the late morning mugginess, cooling her through her sweat-dampened linen tunic and trousers.

She loved it here, planet side on Ellis. Loved this lagoon.

Dark estuary waters, pungent with life, eels and fish and seaweed, flowed around the cantilevered roots of the mangrove. Her mangrove was one of the multitude of trees in the mangrove-filled estuary along the western edge of the lagoon. The lagoon was protected by a several-kilometer long crescent shaped reef of coral opposite the estuary, with clear water ranging from amber by the mangroves to brilliant turquoise darkening to indigo in the center. A narrow channel in the crescent allowed access to the ocean.

The lagoon was the most beautiful place on Ellis.

She hated when she had to leave. But according to the Species Conservation Convention, or SCC, by-laws, the colonists couldn't live full time on the planet until Geo Mining Works, the company that had purchased the right to settle Ellis and its two moons a century ago, fully assessed any possible impacts. Killaine's work with the sea rhinos, those glorious cetacean / pinnipeds analogues that she discovered as child, was a critical part of that assessment.

The colonists lived comfortably within a system of domes on the near moon, Mayros, and supported itself by mining minerals from the larger, more distant, moon, Calcoun. They didn't have to go planet side. Some of the original settlers were aging happily in the domes, content to just observe Ellis from afar.

Killaine couldn't live like that. Just couldn't. She needed sky. Wind. And above all, water.

And on the topic of water...Killaine would love to go for a quick swim in the lagoon, but planet side rules stated absolutely no solo swims, not even mid-day.

As idyllic as Ellis seemed, predators swam in the waters. Predators to whom someone like Killaine would be a tasty snack. The colonists had lost two people early on, eaten by the large sinuous serpents that hunted around the mangroves.

Fieldwork=patience, she doodled on the recorder, using her fingertip instead of a stylus. *Not impulsiveness*. How many times had her mother tried to teach her that? Even after twenty plus years of her own independent work, her mother's restrictiveness popped up its intrusive head.

She sketched the torpedo-shaped body of a sea rhino next. Fixed, backwards-facing rear flippers, more flexible front flippers. A long power tail. And the head: a chiseled, full brow and rounded skull, room for a big brain. The tusk-like horn growing upward from the tip of its nose, and one more, shorter, between its nose and its brow ridge.

As a child, trailing after her marine biologist mother Sarah, Killaine had been the first human to spot a sea rhino. And name them.

She filled in the details of her sketch. Huge dark eyes, set forward in their skulls; the eye position of a predator, though Killaine had never observed them hunting in all her years of fieldwork. The bristly whiskers of the snout.

Added the water ripple pattern of dark blue, light blue, and cream along the dorsum, and pale cream across the belly.

The sea rhinos were beautiful, their color suiting the balmy tropics of Ellis.

The older sea rhinos were criss-crossed with pale scars, each with their own recognizable pattern. She drew the scars than her favorite, Canna, bore.

An objective scientist wouldn't name her subjects. Her mother taught her that, painstakingly numbering each individual creature she logged, along with a description, everything that could identify that individual.

Of course Killaine gave the sea rhinos names, not numbers.

Dana, the matriarch, the bristles of her muzzle grizzled with age, her back white with scars. Liz and May. Jill, the baby. Joe and Brad, the shy males.

And Canna, Dana's daughter. Killaine's best friend, the first sea rhino she met. By Killaine's guess, about her own age in sea rhino years. Maturing along with her, yes, but with a recklessness akin to Killaine's own.

Somehow, Canna always knew when Killaine landed planet side, and within hours of Killaine's arrival, Canna would meet her at the mangrove.

Killaine had initially tried, she really had, to not view the sea rhinos anthropomorphically, but after spending her adult life studying this pod, gaining their trust, earning their friendship...they were people to her. Closer, really, than anyone she knew on Mayros outside of her mother, since her father had passed away five years ago.

This lagoon, this mangrove, was *home*, sticky sap and all, more than her small cozy dome side apartment on Mayros with its top level view.

She could tell when the sea rhinos were happy. Sad. Content. Joyful. And they picked up her moods, too.

And then...Killaine didn't tell anyone, especially not her mom, but over the years, subjective, not objective, *observing* had evolved into *interaction*. Swimming together. Exploring the estuary.

Initiated by the sea rhinos. By Canna. Not her. That was Killaine's only defense.

EVERYTHING KILLAINE KNEW of Earth and Earth creatures, was out of vids and texts. She studied everything about Earth cetaceans and pinnipeds, searching for anything that helped her better understand the sea rhinos.

She'd learned a lot, and not enough.

Sea rhinos lived in small matriarchal family groups. Juvenile males left and formed cohorts of their own, until they found another group to join. The juvenile females would live with their mothers and grandmothers, and maybe even great and great-great grandmothers.

Killaine still wasn't sure how long the sea rhinos lived.

This sort of matriarchal society was common in many of the larger Earth cetacean species: Orcas, sperm whales, and so on. It wasn't typical of pinnipeds, which the sea rhinos more superficially resembled.

The youngest of the calves, Jill, was five years old. Her birth was the first, and only, sea rhino birth Killaine, or any other human, had witnessed.

With their long lives, Killaine didn't expect them to have babies often. She still didn't have a good grasp of gestation time, but expected it was long, maybe even a year or more, based on the size of the sea rhinos; adult females were up to three meters long, tip of the nose to tip of the tail flukes. Males were just a bit smaller.

The sea rhinos sang while they mated, fluting voices that warbled with pleasure and contentment.

Liz was pregnant with Brad's calf, Killaine just knew it.

Killaine had never wanted children of her own, but she felt the joy and anticipation of the pod, looking forward to adding a new member.

Soon. Soon Liz would give birth. All Killaine had to do was be patient.

Canna, right on time, swam up to the mangrove and chirped up at her. The rest of the pod splashed in the open area, away from the mangroves, in deeper water.

Killaine wasn't swimming alone if she was swimming with her friend Canna.

Not by how Killaine interpreted the rules.

She slipped off her tunic and pants, and draped them neatly over the branch in front of her. She hung her recorder by her sandals. And dove, slicing cleanly into the tea-colored water.

Canna splashed her with one broad flipper as Killaine surfaced. The sea rhino exhaled softly, rapidly. Laughing at her. Killaine splashed back, less effectively with her small hands, and Canna chuffed harder, her nostril slits flaring.

Then Canna quieted. Looked so serious, so grave, with her dear face scrunched up, bristles quivering, Killaine thought she'd done something wrong.

"Canna?" she said, treading water. "Canna, what's wrong?"

She felt a thrum deep in her belly, a vibration against her ribs. Canna looked frustrated, then apologetic.

And then Canna *bit* Killaine's hand with her sharp incisors. And everything turned to rainbows.

———

KILLAINE? Sister? Wake up, Killaine. Canna's voice. What she'd always imagined Canna would sound like, if she could speak like a human.

Killaine was still in the water, Joe and Liz and Brad supporting her as she lay across their backs in the center of the lagoon. It was late afternoon, and she could barely see Mayros on the horizon through the haze of moisture.

She couldn't see the bottom of the lagoon. The water was fairly clear, blue green rather than the mangrove-stained amber, but it was so deep she just saw darkness. No sand, no sea grass. She was in the deepest area. She'd never swum so far out from the mangroves.

"Canna?" Her lips were dry. Cracked. She licked them, the umami richness of the dried lagoon salts filling her mouth.

Oh, good, Canna said. *It worked.*

Dana loomed behind her, radiating disapproval. *And if it hadn't?* she said. Stern. No nonsense.

Alpha bitch, Killaine thought, and Canna chuffed.

Oops. She'd said that good as out loud.

Worth it, Canna said, and Killaine reached for her flipper in reassurance.

"How?" Killaine was going to have to work on saying more than one word at a time, but her bitten hand still ached and she was still seeing rainbows out of her peripheral vision.

Eels swam into view beneath her, their long undulating bodies lazy and relaxed.

Relax. She needed to relax. She was safe with Canna and the pod. She was. She trusted Canna.

Even if she had bitten her.

Sorry. I wanted to be able to really talk to you.

How—what—?

I figured out an enzyme to edit you, Canna said. *You're still you, but more.*

You could have killed her, snapped Dana. *You did not ask permission.*

I couldn't! She wasn't able to understand me!

Just because you can do something, doesn't mean you have the right to do it, Dana said, echoing Killaine's earlier thoughts.

It's okay, Killaine said. *I would've said yes.*

Her mother had always despaired of Killaine's lack of impartiality, her recklessness.

If she'd told you you'll never be able to leave, to go back to your habitat?

I heard her! She said here *was home!*

I can't go back to Mayros?

I'm sorry. No. Canna. Contrite.

Killaine trembled. Anger? Fear? Shock? She couldn't say. All of those emotions, tangled up. Knotting her stomach. Her head ached and she didn't know if it was because she was changing, still, or just because her blood pressure had shot sky high.

She slipped off the sea rhinos and dove into the deep water, stroking with her arms, arms that seemed shorter and thicker, hands broader. Dolphin kicking with legs that propelled her ten meters down without her even really trying.

She stopped, then, in the shadow of the sea rhinos still floating on the surface. An eel slipped by her, rubbing itself against her calves like a cat, then swam on. She could *see*, clearer than she ever had underwater, even with a diving mask. Motes of tiny planktonic material, creatures, glittering in the sunlight that penetrated to this level. Darkness below, but she could perceive shapes, the mounds of rocks studding the floor of the lagoon, the long strands of dark seagrass fuzzing the sand, thirty or so meters down. As she gazed, her vision adjusted, and she saw more detail. The sea grass, limned with phosphorescent cilia, flickered with iridescence. Crystals in the rocks reflected the dimming sunlight with a soft blue light. More tiny creatures, each with its own spark of light. Of life.

It's beautiful. Killaine swam deeper. Down to the sea grass. The movement of the cilia along the edges was mesmerizing.

Canna joined her, her big body graceful and swift. *It is, isn't it? Watch.* Canna grabbed a mouthful of sea grass and chewed. *Try it.*

Killaine reached for a strand.

Just bite.

She leaned towards the strand. Nibbled. It was spicy, peppery, firm on the outside, but filled with a sweet tangy liquid that burst in her mouth as she chewed. *It's good.*

One of the mainstays of our diet this time of year. Then, plaintively: *Forgive me?*

Killaine rolled over to face Canna. The sea rhino's eyes were wide, the pupils dilated. Killaine could see herself reflected in them, the changes Canna's enzyme had already wrought. Her own dark eyes, huge in her thin face, pupils so dilated only the hint of brown iris flickered; her thickening torso, her shortening arms. And gills, gills she didn't even know the sea rhinos had, fluttering like butterflies along her rib cage. *Will I look like you?*

Enough to swim with us.

Swimming meant living.

And you'll stay human enough to talk to the humans.

Killaine could just imagine what would happen to Ellis and the sea rhinos, if the colony wasn't adhering to the SCC, and information about this got out. Humans had the ability to fine tune DNA, but not to change an adult into something so radically different. Maybe, if surgery was involved, but Killaine knew Canna had changed the very essence of her DNA, so much that her old body was morphing into something new, some hybrid of sea rhino and human.

A real mermaid.

We don't use it much, Canna said. *Just when we break. Or need to change.*

The sea rhinos (and that name seemed so undignified, now) were wildly beyond human tech.

Serro, Canna said. *We call ourselves the Serro. So you were close, calling us sea rhinos, just interpreting it as made sense to you. That's why I thought this would work. You know us better than you thought. You'd already been communicating, learning, without realizing it.*

So I'm your link to humans. She nibbled on another stalk of sea grass.

A friend, foremost. And a valued member of the pod. And I hope, yes, you will be a liaison to the humans.

Already Canna considered Killaine one of them, the Serro, not a human. How deep did the changes go?

As deep as you want.

By sunset, Killaine returned to the mangrove. She climbed it awkwardly, her limbs already more suited to the water than terrestrial life, and retrieved her clothing and recorder.

The shirt sleeves were too long and too tight. The pants were too long and too tight, especially across her thighs. But she didn't want to report back nude, and she had nothing else to wear. She ripped the side seams of her shirt open to just under her armpits so she could breathe without risk of tearing the fabric, her new blunt claws making short work of the job. Better.

The clothing felt rough against her skin. Wrong. She wanted to rip it off and dive back into the water.

"I'll be back tomorrow," she promised Canna. She'd hike to her campsite, radio her mother. Tell her what happened.

Ask her mom's advice. Killaine couldn't just disappear, much as she wanted to.

Hello. This is your daughter, the mermaid. The siren. The chimera of an alien species and a human. She traced the bones of her face: nose, cheekbones, chin. Her face was still human. Ish. Human-ish.

She'd never had a child of her own, a grandchild for her mother. Now she wouldn't. Oh, she'd banked eggs as required, so maybe someone would decide to access her original DNA, use it for themselves, keep the genetics of the colony diverse. But now, she'd never, ever bear one herself.

She'd never wanted to, but now she had no choice. And she felt a loss she never thought she'd suffer.

She still didn't want a child.

But she wanted the *choice*.

Help Liz. She could help Liz with her baby. Her calf. Help the pod raise its new member. Focus on that.

Killaine hiked the half kilometer back to her campsite, leg muscles cramping uncomfortably. She could feel her bones shortening, resculpting, even as she walked. The jasmine smelled sharper, more pungent, than it ever had, tickling her nose. And the breeze...she could taste things, spoors, pollens, against her skin. She wondered if she would be able to read scent on the currents with her skin, if she were in the lagoon.

She'd set up her tent, a lightweight contraption of aluminum poles and linen canvas, on a hummock of turf, surrounded by more mangroves (a different species, one that liked dryer roots), that morning.

Twelve hours ago.

Twelve hours, before her entire life had changed.

She had tucked the small comms radio, nothing high tech, just strong enough to reach her mom on a narrow channel, in her silk sleep-sack in the tent.

Her legs seized up and she fell, biting back a scream. It *hurt*, worse than when she'd broke her arm climbing mangroves to the tippy top branches, despite her mother yelling at her to climb back down.

The spasms lasted only a few seconds.

She panted in relief.

Spending the night at the campsite, in the tent, didn't seem like a good idea anymore.

She retrieved the radio, tuned it to her mom's private channel. She heard crackling, then her mom's soft rich voice.

"Killaine? Is everything alright, honey?"

Nearly forty years old, and Killaine would always be her mom's little girl, despite all the disagreements. Killaine swiped at her face. *Crying? I'm not crying. Not me. Not tough mermaid me.*

"Mom?"

"What's wrong?" Her mother's voice sharpened.

"I—something's happened." How did you explain something like this?

You didn't. You just said it.

"Canna bit me and now I'm turning into a sea rhino. A Serro." Crackling.

"They create an enzyme that alters DNA. That can alter our DNA. And they want me as a liaison, between them and the humans."

"Canna bit you."

"Yes. Mom, I'm still me, but I'm going to live with them."

"You're at your regular site?"

"Yes. But Mom, I have to go to the lagoon. I can't sleep here. I'm changing. I need to be in the water."

"I'll come to the lagoon tomorrow." Her mom disconnected.

———

KILLAINE PACKED UP THE TENT, all her gear. Her clothes. Her sandals. Shoved it all into her backpack and hung it from a low hanging branch to keep it safe, while she still could, before her fingers shortened into clawed nubs.

Her throat was raw after the last episode of cramping.

What had Canna said? How much would Killaine change? Just as much as she wanted?

Well, she wanted to keep her hands, damn it. Claws, fine, webbing, sure. But she wanted the dexterity of hands.

She stumbled back to the lagoon.

Canna was waiting.

———

THE NEXT MORNING, Killaine woke as soon as the sun rose, swimming to the surface with powerful strokes of her back flippers, extending her arms—with thumbs! and webbed fingers!—in front, tasting the location and numbers of eels, of fish, of a myriad of other creatures she'd never known lived in the lagoon, all through her sensitive skin. Further in the distance, far enough away to be no danger, she sensed the acrid bitterness of the immense serpents, twining through the mangrove roots.

The bright sunlight sunspotted her eyes as she burst through the surface. Her pupils narrowed to pinpricks. She could see that her skin, formerly a rich tan, now resembled sunlight filtered through mangrove branches. Her claws gleamed at the ends of her fingertips.

She inhaled. Caught a whiff of...human...

Mom. She surged towards the mangrove estuary.

Canna followed her.

Her mom waited at Killaine's mangrove, sitting on one of the lower roots, linen trousers rolled up, narrow feet bare, trailing her toes along the surface of the water. Her mom looked frail, perched on the massive root, but when Killaine awkwardly pulled herself onto land, struggling to stand straight, her mom hauled her upright.

"Oh, honey," her mom said, hugging her.

Killaine hugged her back, careful of the strength in her arms.

Canna hung back, silent.

"What do you think?" Killaine asked.

Her mom sighed. "You've always jumped first, never looking ahead. I'm scared. I don't want to lose you. It's horrible, and magnificent, and the scientist in me knows if I was even twenty years younger I'd be living down here to watch and see what happens.

"But as a mother, I'm angry." Her mom glared at Canna. "They didn't give you any choice."

"I think I would've agreed."

"But you didn't get a choice."

Canna trilled. *Tell her I'm sorry, but I had to. I had no true choice, either. We are at a point, the Serro and humans, that we need to be able to clearly communicate.*

"Canna's sorry, she really is. But she thinks it's time we all talked."

Her mom glared at Canna.

"Mom, just think. If they could do this to me, what else could they have done over the years? They've shown remarkable restraint, really. More than humans have. And I'm okay with it. Just think of everything I'll be able to learn."

"Would the Serro send one of theirs to us?" her mom asked. "Modify one of their own?"

Canna stilled. *If it was required.*

"Mom...we came here. Trying to step as lightly as possible, but we're the invaders. Not them."

Her mom sighed. "You've always been stubborn."

Killaine's chest tightened. "I love you, mom."

"Love you too, kiddo." Her mom stepped back. "I'm going back to Mayros to start laying the groundwork for all this. You've brought me out of retirement and into politics. Meet me here in a week?"

Killaine nodded. "Sounds good."

Her mom hugged her once more. Kissed her forehead. Looked at Canna. "Take care of her," she said gruffly, then left.

———

SIX MONTHS LATER, Killaine swam to the mangrove. Canna swam with her, as did Liz.

And Liz's new baby calf, pale blue and fuzzy all over. He was already a strong fearless swimmer. And he wanted to meet a human.

And after he met Killaine's mom, after they returned to the center of the lagoon, he couldn't stop squeaking about how he would visit Mayros when he was old enough.

This may just work out, Killaine said to Canna. *It just might work out.*

Canna chuffed.

ABOUT THE AUTHOR

Since graduating from West Point, Stephannie Tallent has served in the Army as a Military Intelligence officer during Desert Storm, gotten a Zoology degree, went to vet school, worked as a small animal veterinarian, and designed and published knitting patterns and books.

Throughout all that she's always wanted to be a writer, and she's finally put all her type A, soft-spoken, invisible middle-aged woman focus on that goal, writing everything from fantasy to science fiction, mysteries and romance.

She has sold stories to Pulphouse Magazine and the WMG Holiday Spectacular.

www.stephannietallent.com

Sign up for Stephannie's newsletter!
https://www.stephannietallent.com/subscribe/

ALSO BY STEPHANNIE TALLENT

Short Story Collections

Gates of Wonder

The Chronicles of Dinah Lee Wright Vol 1

The Chronicles of Dinah Lee Wright Vol 2

Gratitude of the Ocean: Jolene Tomberlin Series

The Serpent in the Shallows: Jolene Tomberlin Series

The Monkey's Journal

The Kaleidoscope Jaguars of the Jungles of Mexicatl

The Mermaid of Ellis Prime

The Alchemy of Science and Mystery

One Plus One Equals More (mystery/crime)

A Snowman Made of Sand (romance)

KnitWitch (fantasy and knitting patterns)